MARLY'S GHOST

A remix of Charles Dickens's
A CHRISTMAS CAROL with a
Valentine's twist

DAVID LEVITHAN

ELECTRIC MONKEY BOOKS BY DAVID LEVITHAN

EVERY DAY

HOW THEY MET AND OTHER STORIES

MARLY'S GHOST

TWO BOYS KISSING

WRITTEN WITH RACHEL COHN

NAOMI AND ELY'S NO KISS LIST

NICK AND NORAH'S INFINITE PLAYLIST

MARLY'S GHOST

I was at my desk now, and my glance happened to come to rest on Marly's old charm bracelet, another gift to me, to remember all the times I'd spun it around her wrist.

One of the charms was a little golden bell. As I watched, it began to shiver. At first it moved so softly that it scarcely made a sound. But soon it rang out loudly—much louder than I would have thought possible. Every other bell, alarm, and tone in the house chimed in, from the microwave downstairs to the doorbell in the hall. A cacophony of bells. This might have lasted half a minute, or a minute, but seemed like an hour. Then the bells ceased all at once, leaving the room in absolute silence.

There came a clanking noise from downstairs. Like heavy chain being dragged. First faintly... then closer. Hitting against the stairs. Dragged across the floor. Coming straight for my room. "This isn't happening," I said to myself. "I refuse to believe this is happening." Too little sleep, too much caffeine, a trick of the light—The flame in the fireplace leaped up and suddenly there was a figure in the door. Walking right through the door. Walking to me. Marly's Ghost.

DAVID LEVITHAN

Illustrated by Brian Selznick

First published in Great Britain in 2015 by Electric Monkey,
an imprint of Egmont UK Limited
The Yellow Building, 1 Nicholas Road, London W11 4AN
Published by arrangement with Dial,
a division of Penguin Young Readers Group,
a member of Penguin Group USA (LLC)

Text copyright © 2006 David Levithan
Illustrations © 2006 Brian Selznick

The moral rights of the author have been asserted

ISBN 978 1 4052 7647 4

59444/1

www.egmont.co.uk

A CIP catalogue record for this title is available from the British Library

Typeset by Avon DataSet Ltd, Bidford on Avon, Warwickshire
Printed and bound in Great Britain by CPI Group

Stay safe online. Any website addresses listed in this book are correct at the time of going
to print. However, Egmont is not responsible for content hosted by third parties.
Please be aware that online content can be subject to change and websites can contain
content that is unsuitable for children. We advise that all children are supervised
when using the internet.

FOR BS & DS
(constant inspirations)

CONTENTS

STAVE I
MARLY'S GHOST

MARLY WAS DEAD, TO BEGIN WITH. There was no doubt whatsoever about that. I had been there. When she went off the treatments, she decided she wanted to die at home, and she wanted me to be there with her family. So I sat, and I waited, and I was destroyed.

There are no metaphors, no words for such a feeling. You are left with no doubt, and endless doubt.

We stood around the bed, counting her breaths, holding our own. Her father held her hand. Her mother sobbed. Her grandmothers prayed. I felt as if I was being undone one stitch at a time. She was sixteen years old, but there in the bed she could have been

3

ninety. Everything about her that had once smiled was now gone. She hadn't been awake for days. The last word I'd said to her was *goodbye* – but I'd meant for the afternoon, not forever. Afterwards, I told her *I love you* so many times it hurt. But I had no way of knowing whether she heard or not.

I repeated it now – *I love you. I love you. Please. I love you.* Then it came – that one small gasp. We waited for the next one, but there was no next one. You expect death to bring some new form of punctuation, but there it is: one small gasp. Period.

I know people say that when you die, your life flashes in front of your eyes. I have no idea what Marly saw. I will never know. But after that last gasp, after that loud silent moment, suddenly our life together flashed before my own eyes. It couldn't have taken longer than ten seconds, but it was all there: our eighth-grade dance, the first time we'd gone out as a couple, doing the box-step in a gymnasium decorated with purple and blue balloons; watching movies together in her den, curling up together under the blanket her aunt had made when Marly was born; meeting at our new high-school lockers, passing notes, sharing books, or simply smiling at the sight of each other; going on double dates with Fred and Sarah, holding hands underneath the table, feeling her charm bracelet press against my wrist; the two of us retreating to the dark of my room, her hand rising under my shirt, my whole life bending over to kiss her; feeling her becoming lighter in my arms as the treatments took more and more and more of her.

It passed so quickly. And when it was gone – when all of it was gone – I was left with nothing. It was as if all the moments had died along with her. Everything had died. Everything except me. And that was arguable. There were times when I felt I had died, too.

When you die, the heart just stops.

When she died, my heart just stopped.

I knew she was dead. In every hour, every minute, every second since that one small gasp, I knew she was dead. How could it be otherwise?

I had known Marly for six years, since we were ten. We had been together for three of those years, until she died, just four months ago.

Her absence was all that mattered to me now, just as her presence had been all that mattered to me then. The people around me measured their days in hours or class periods or meals. I used to measure the days in glimpses of her face, touches from her hand, words sent back and forth through the air, all the things I'd tell her. I had never before experienced a love so elemental. And I never would again.

B&M

We had carved it everywhere. The trees where we walked. The benches where we sat. On the bedposts. The walls. Still there, every time I looked. There was no way to erase her without removing myself.

I was what remained. And that's what my life felt like: remaining. I went through the motions. I drowned myself in homework and tests. I pushed myself as fast as I could through each day. I tried not to look too closely at anyone else, because they had what I'd lost – seeing them touch, seeing them happy made me bitter, jealous, sad. I was old at a young age – I knew things that nobody around me knew. I knew the truth of grief, the truth of watching a person slowly die, the angry emptiness of still being around. I made myself hard and sharp. I became secret and self-contained. Solitary.

This was not a choice. It was what I had to do.

The cold within me froze my features, made my eyes red, my thin lips blue, and spoke out in a voice that grated in my own ears. I iced the air wherever I went. I chilled all the conversations.

Love was to blame for this. Because when love ends, the cold is what you're left with.

It was all I needed to feel.

Life goes on. Get over it. You're still young. It'll get better. Blah blah blah. At first people had tried to draw me in and draw me out. My friends tried to make me return to a world where there were colors besides black and gray, gave me consolations and invitations and conversations that grew more and more one-sided as my side shut down. There was no way to explain to them how I felt, because if they'd been able to understand, there wouldn't have been any need to explain. I knew some of them loved her – genuinely loved her. But not in the way I had. I knew they were grieving, too, but I needed distance for my own grief. I chose to edge my way along the crowded paths of life, keeping sympathy away. I didn't want it. I didn't need it. I wanted and needed Marly, and she was gone.

I wanted to die.

That Friday, that day before Valentine's Day, was no different. I walked through the hallways of our school and paid as little attention as I could to the stamping and wheezing and talking around me. Some lockers were decked out with construction-paper hearts – to me, the only thing they had in common with real hearts was their ability to be torn so easily. Black hearts – I wanted to see black hearts in the halls, hearts that smelled like smoke and weighed as much as sadness. While everyone else focused on their boyfriends and girlfriends, on roses and carnations and *dates*, I looked out the windows at the bleak midwinter. The last bell of the day had just rung, but it was quite dark already, with a fog covering the parking lot and the football field and the town beyond. I wanted to be out there, evaporating.

But I couldn't disappear if people kept finding me. I couldn't make it through the halls without being stopped by some bright-colored remnant of my past life.

"Happy almost-Valentine's Day!" my onetime best friend Fred called out, coming upon me so quickly that I had no chance to avoid him. Hope still flickered in his voice – I couldn't figure out a way to extinguish it. I was not in the mood for him, or the ghost of our friendship, or talk about Valentine's Day and love.

"Love is humbug," I said to him.

He was all in a glow, his eyes sparkling.

"'Love is humbug'!" he repeated. "You can't possibly mean that."

He wanted me to play along, to banter. But I couldn't do that anymore. I'd lost that.

After somebody dies, you find that everybody else's old roles amplify. Fred had always been the one to keep us together, to rally us and cheer us. I knew he missed Marly, and I knew that somewhere underneath his gestures of happiness, he was sad. But my role had simply been to love her, and now that amplified itself in clear, lucid pain. No holiday, no talk of love, could change that.

"I *do* mean it," I said, unable to keep the frost from my voice. Then, seeing he still didn't believe me, I added, "I'm sick and tired of all this useless energy spent on love. All the drama. All the expectation. All these couples pretending to fit together because that's what they think they're supposed to do. I am sick of *celebrating* that. I am sick of glorifying the vulnerability and codependency of dimwitted lonely people who spend thirty dollars on a dozen roses and think that means something more than a waste of money."

"Come on, Ben." Fred looked at me with sad sympathy. The exact wrong thing to do. "You have to lighten up a little."

"How can I lighten up," I said darkly, "when everyone around me is so deluded? Everyone thinks that what they're experiencing is real. That it will last. What's Valentine's Day about except the desperate search to find someone to spend Valentine's Day with? It just shows that love has become a marketing campaign, like everything else. You buy into it and lose everything. If I had my way, I would force everyone who sings out 'Happy Valentine's Day' to eat a thousand candy hearts without water, and then lock them in a heart-shaped box until they came out sane."

"Ben!" Fred pleaded.

"Fred!" I returned sarcastically. "Go do Valentine's Day your way and I'll do it mine."

"I don't care about the holiday," Fred said. "I care about you. You're making it sound like you've abandoned the whole concept of love."

"Let me abandon it, then. Love and I once had a great relationship, but I fear we've broken up. It cheated on me, wrecked my heart, and then went on to date other people. *A lot* of other people. And I can't stand to watch it, since love's going to cheat on them too. Just watch."

Fred put his hand on my shoulder and it took every ounce of my restraint not to shrink away from his touch.

11

"I know it's hard," he began. And I couldn't let him go on. This time I pulled away. Even when he tried to keep the hand there, tried to keep hold.

"If you don't shut up," I warned, "I'm leaving. Save the love talk for when Hallmark needs your advice."

Stop it, Marly said, somewhere in my head. *He's your friend.*

Fred's hand dropped to his side. "Don't be angry, Ben. I didn't mean anything. It's just – at least tell me you'll come over tomorrow for the party. We really want you there."

A party. Another place she wouldn't be. Another place for me to sit and watch, remaining. A party I would chill to its core.

Fred and Sarah laughing. Exchanging gifts. Holding hands.

The continuing half of the double date.

"I don't think so," I said. "The last place I want to be is a Valentine's gathering with you and Sarah."

"It's an *anti*-Valentine party. There will be other people there."

"And *Sarah*," I said, speaking her name like a curse. Not because I disliked her, but because I disliked *them*.

"What do you have against Sarah?" Fred asked.

I sighed. There was no use going into it, because it was so twisted. Every time I saw them together, I was angry at them for being together. And at the same time, I pictured how broken he'd be when it was over. How thoroughly shot.

"Why did you start going out with her?" I asked.

"Because I fell in love."

"Because you fell in love!" I laughed. "How *easy* for you!"

I hit the mark, and stopped Fred for a second. Then he collected himself and said, "It's not Sarah that's keeping you away. You haven't hung out with me or anyone else, really, since . . ."

He wouldn't finish the sentence, letting the last words hang in the haunted realm of the unsaid.

"Since what?" I asked cruelly.

"You know what, Ben . . . Why can't we be friends?"

"I have to go," I said. And it was the truth – it was as if I would slip off the edge entirely if I had to stay for one more sentence, one more attempt.

But not Fred. He always had to leave on good terms.

"I'm sorry, with all my heart, to see you like this," he told me. "I swear to God, if I knew how to make you snap out of it, I would. Do you really think this is what she would have wanted? Do you really think this is the right way to go? You don't even fight with me. You can't even be bothered to do that. You think if you keep turning us down and turning us away that we'll give up. And maybe you're right. Maybe that's what some people have done, and others will do. But I'm not going to stop caring about you, my friend. I'm not going to stop believing in love because of what happened. I can't. And you shouldn't either."

I should have been a little moved. I should have thawed just a little bit.

But I could feel myself missing her even more. I could see her there at the party, joking with Sarah about the appropriate anti-Valentine decorations, telling Fred he looked charming in whatever he chose to wear. I could feel her warmth on the couch next to me. I could see her telling me she didn't want a drink, then spending the night sipping from mine. I could hear her laugh. For last year's anti-Valentine's Day party, she'd dressed up as a beekeeper because she'd discovered that, besides being the patron saint of love and lovers, Saint Valentine was also a patron saint of beekeepers, epilepsy, fainting, and plague.

"Beekeeper," she'd said, *"seemed like the best option."*

She had lost a lot of her energy by then, so we propped her up on garish cupid pillows and acted out the story of Saint Valentine (quickly researched on the Internet) for her. If she was the beekeeper, we were all her willing hive. We showed Saint Valentine healing the blind, counseling the imprisoned until Claudius II (played with relish by Sarah) ordered him to renounce his faith. We ended with him being beaten not by clubs but by leftover candy canes, and staged his beheading using a marsh- mallow Peep.

I remembered how Marly had laughed, with me (out of the play early after playing the no-longer-blind girl) at her side. And then the laugh dissolved in the present. And the drink that I wanted to offer her in the future went untouched. And the warmth turned back to cold. I could not thaw, not even for Fred.

I looked him in the eye with all the sad and bitter coldness I felt, and I said it again: "I have to go."

If I were in his place, I would have given up on me. But instead he left without an angry word.

I felt certain that he'd be thankful, later on, that I'd let him go.

I thought I would be free to leave now. The Valentine's Day buzz was enclosing me more and more in a brooding claustrophobia. I had suffered through one conversation, and that had been more than enough. Marly and I used to play this game together – we called it dodgehall, and it involved running to our lockers after school, getting the books we needed, and getting out of the building before anyone else could stop us from having our time alone together. Because as much as we liked our friends, the minute our day turned from school to free time we wanted to spend that freedom on each other. All the other conversations were side conversations. All the other encounters were obstacles. We would race, and our hearts would skip, and whoever dodged through the halls the slowest would have to buy the ice cream, or finish the homework, or be the one to invent the lie we'd tell our parents when we got home late.

Of course, everything changed when she got sick. The obstacles were ones we couldn't run past. We just had to arrange our lives around them. So we did.

I thought I could escape the school without being stopped again. But when I was at my locker, unloading my books, I was accosted by two boys with two armloads of flowers. They were both freshmen, and I only knew their names because our school didn't have that many pairs of freshmen boyfriends. One was short and hesitant, the other tall, lanky, and hesitant.

"Would you like to buy a carnation?" Tiny asked meekly.

"The proceeds go to Key Club," Tim quietly chimed in.

"I'm allergic," I told them flatly.

"You could give one to your girlfriend," Tiny offered.

"Or your boyfriend," Tim said even more quietly.

"My girlfriend died four months ago," I replied

curtly. "And I don't have a boyfriend."

"I'm sorry," Tiny said.

"That's awful," Tim seconded.

"You have no idea," I said, standing now and facing them. I did not appreciate their invasion of my space. I fell out of the hold of whatever had been keeping me from lashing out. I was as tall as Tim, so much taller than Tiny. They wilted a little as I spoke. "You have no idea about anything, do you? How long have you been together?"

"Two months," Tiny answered.

"And four days," Tim added.

"Let me tell you right now – that's *nothing*. You could plant *fields* of carnations for each other, and that won't prevent what's going to happen. You think you're in love? You think it's even *possible* for you to be in love? I'm going to tell you something, for your own good. Then you can decide whether or not to give me a flower in return. There is no such thing as 'in love.' Love is not something you can ever get inside of. You might think you're there. Sure. But then you hit the border and realize you've been outside the whole time."

18

I looked at Tiny and pointed to Tim. "I don't know how it will end," I told Tiny. "Maybe he'll find someone more attractive than you. He'll cheat on you. He'll lie to you. He'll swear that it's love." I looked at Tim and pointed to Tiny. "And maybe he'll leave you in a different way. He'll grow distant. He'll become a mystery you can't solve. Or maybe something else will intervene. He'll need you more than you can bear. It will be too much, and because it's too much you'll know that you never really made it *in* love. You couldn't push far enough to be *in*."

They just stood there for a second, shocked. Then Tim, mumbling down to his flowers, said, "White is for friendship, pink is for crushes, and red is for love. Which do you want?"

"I want this all to be over – is that really so hard to understand? I don't want to have anything to do with anyone. As far as I'm concerned, nobody else exists!"

"Sorry," Tiny said, wiping his eyes. Then, seeing that it would be useless to pursue their point, he leaned into Tim and they both moved away.

♥ ♥ ♥

The fog and the darkness outside thickened. But when I stepped into it, I couldn't disappear completely. I could still see the things immediately around me – buses the color of caution lights, smokers on the front steps cupping their hands for fire. It was only the distance that was blotted out. Not my footsteps. Not my clouded breathing. Not my thoughts.

What did it feel like to touch her skin? What was our biggest fight? What were the exact words she said when she told me she'd go out with me? What else will I forget?

Marly, in my mind, said, *Stop it.*

But if I stop it, it's over, I argued. I knew she wouldn't want it to be over.

The church tower was invisible now, but it still rang out in the clouds, once every fifteen minutes. I felt the vibrations of time as I walked on, the railings of the graveyard now beside me. I kept walking, even though Marly was there. Her resting place, because it contained the rest of her, her remains. The things I loved were gone, and no coffin, no marker could preserve them.

Foggier yet, and colder. Piercing, searching, biting cold.

Picturing her crying. Feeling her tears soak into her shirt. Knowing there was nothing, nothing that I could do.

Having her scream at me – *Go away*. Having her tell me she was all alone, that there was no way for me to understand how that felt. Telling me to leave, but letting me back in after a phone call, a note, a day passing.

I plunged past, into town. A loving couple loitered across the sidewalk in front of me, holding hands, nestling against the cold. I had to run into the street to get around them. I wanted to yell.

Her voice in my head: *There should be a minimum speed limit for people in love walking on the sidewalk. They're worse than moms with strollers.* Or maybe just my own voice in my head, disguised as hers.

I passed the park with the playground swings and the diner with the jukebox booths. The trees we'd vowed to climb and the benches where we would sit reading next to each other, her arm pressed so closely against mine that I'd feel it when she turned a page. All of the places that had been bled of purpose. I couldn't feel anything for them anymore, except loss. The past was ruined for me.

My parents were away for the weekend, so I stopped at a quiet, forlorn deli far enough into the outskirts of our small suburban town to be private. I sat at one of the two tables and single-mindedly plied through my homework and ate food without taste. The light was fluorescent. No music played. That was all right with me.

When I was done there, I took a shortcut through a thick veil of trees to get to my house. Closer to the center of town, the houses kept one another company, the doorways only a conversational distance apart. Here, however, the houses kept to themselves. Ours was an old and dreary recluse – I hadn't even liked it as a kid. Even though I knew every step of the shortcut, every step of the yard, I found myself groping through the darkness that had set in, so full of frost and fog. I made it up the front steps and had just put my key in the lock when I stopped and looked at the old knocker on the door.

There was nothing at all particular about the knocker, except that it was very large. It had been on the door for as long as we'd lived in the house, which in my case was as long as I'd been alive. I had walked past the knocker for years without seeing it, or caring if it saw me. But this time something made me stop. Something made me look. One moment it was just the ordinary knocker. And the next moment it was . . .

Marly's face.

It was not in impenetrable shadow, as the other objects in the yard were, but had a dismal light around it, like the lowest flame on a gas range. It wasn't angry or ferocious, but looked exactly like she used to look when she'd stop in the middle of studying to talk to me, her glasses turned up on her forehead. Her hair was stirred, as if by breath or hot air, and though her eyes were wide open, they didn't move. That, and the shock of seeing the startling blue of her eyes again, made it horrible. But the horror seemed to be on my side, not hers.

Before I could even gasp, she was gone.

I'd seen her before, of course. I saw her all the time.

Looking out the window in class, I would see her walking across the front lawn, and I would want to jump out of my seat and pound on the glass to call for her. Then she'd come a little closer and it wouldn't be her at all. Just another blond girl on her way to school. A stranger.

Or I'd imagine her. Close my eyes and run the memories of us. See her laughing next to me on my bed. See her pointing out my mismatched socks, amused. Catch her face out of the many in the hallway, see her smile connect as she found me finding her. All these memories were silent. But often that was enough. I would talk back to her, even if I couldn't hear what she was saying.

I tried to convince myself that this was just another one of those sightings. Those imaginings. That fiction.

But still, I *did* pause before I shut the door. And I *did* look cautiously behind it first, as if I half expected to find her there, waiting for me. But there was nothing on the back of the door but the screws and nuts that held the knocker in place. I told myself to get a grip and closed the door with a bang.

The sound resounded through the house like thunder. Every room, from attic to basement, seemed to have its own peal of echoes.

I convinced myself this was normal. Nothing to be afraid of.

I didn't turn on any lights as I walked upstairs to my room. Darkness was solitary, and I liked it. During that brief flicker of her face, I had felt I wasn't alone. I needed the darkness to erase that feeling. Because it *was* a feeling, and I preferred not to feel.

Still, the presence nagged at me. Like a complete fool, I checked under my bed when I got to my room, then opened my closet and took a quick peek between the hanging clothes. Nothing was out of the ordinary. I saw her jacket hanging there and instinctively reached out to touch it – the yellow tattered jacket she'd wanted me to keep, knowing I'd have no use for it except as something to remember her by.

I walked over to the fireplace in my room, which my parents only let me use on cold nights. I checked that the flue was open, then lit the log. A low fire began to burn.

There had been one night, not that long ago, when the memories of Marly had been too much. I had grabbed the tattered shoebox containing our notes and letters, determined to do some harm. I took the top letter and touched it to the flame. I watched it burn for about five seconds before I realized what I was doing and desperately tried to stop it. Too late.

The fireplace was an old one, paved all around with tiles. Blank white tiles . . . which now, as I watched, began to be scribbled with words. Marly's handwriting. The letter I had burned, returned to me now, scrawled across the porcelain.

"No!" I gasped, blinking hard and pulling away. A thousand justifications volunteered themselves in my mind – too little sleep, too much caffeine, a trick of the light. But my fear only grew.

From the other side of the room, it looked like the writing had faded away. I was at my desk now, and my glance happened to come to rest on Marly's old charm bracelet, another last gift to me, to remember all the times I'd spun it around her wrist. One of the charms was a little golden bell. As I watched, it began to shiver. At first it moved so softly that it scarcely made a sound. But soon it rang out loudly – much louder than I would have thought possible. Every other bell, alarm, and tone in the house chimed in, from the microwave downstairs to the doorbell in the hall. A cacophony of bells.

This might have lasted half a minute, or a minute, but it seemed like an hour. Then the bells ceased all at once, leaving the room in absolute silence. There came a clanking noise from downstairs. Like a heavy chain being dragged. First faintly . . . then closer. Hitting against the stairs. Dragged across the floor. Coming straight for my room.

"This isn't happening," I said to myself. "I refuse to believe this is happening."

Too little sleep, too much caffeine, a trick of the light –

The flame in the fireplace leaped up and suddenly there was a figure in the door. Walking right through the door. Walking to me.

Marly's ghost.

The same face. The very same. Whenever I closed my

eyes, I saw it. But now my eyes were open, witnessing her familiar skin, her bluest eyes, her favorite green shirt, and her favorite pair of Saturday night jeans. The shoes I had bought her for our first real Valentine's Day – the shoes she had wanted since the summer before. I would've recognized her anywhere, but I'd never imagined I would be recognizing her in this translucent way.

The chain she dragged was around her waist. Stunned beyond comprehension, I saw it was an elongated version of the charm bracelet, with objects from our life clasped to each link. Not just the golden bell and the golden house and the golden heart from the real bracelet, but books I had given her, flowers from holidays, blankets shared after sex. All of the notes and letters from the shoebox I kept, and all the notes and letters from the shoebox still somewhere in her room. Photographs I could not bear to look at. Her smiling face, even after the treatments had begun.

The chain was solid, but Marly was not. Even though I could see her, I could also see the door behind her. I couldn't believe it. I couldn't believe she was here

in any form, even though she was standing right in front of me, even though I could see the way the blue in her eyes was partly frozen, even though my own eyes could mark the very texture of the folded scarf bound around her head.

It was a dream – or a nightmare – and I would not give in to it.

"What the – !" I said. "What do you want with me?"

"Much," she replied. It was her voice, no doubt about it. And I knew the tone – the same tone she'd have when we whispered in the dark, lying together like folded leaves.

"Who are you?" I asked, even though I knew.

"Ask me who I *was*," she replied. Like we were playing a game.

A cruel trick. My mind was playing a cruel trick.

"Who were you, then?" I murmured.

"Marly."

She seemed so alone. I remembered all those unguarded moments I had stumbled across, seeing her before she saw me, watching her concern as she studied herself in a mirror, witnessing her nervousness every time she met someone new. She had never been fully comfortable with herself, had never trusted things to turn out right. She had been lost on her own and I had been lost on my own, so it was natural that once we found each other we wanted to keep being unlost with each other. Because that, at heart, had made us exist.

I looked to my nightstand and saw the clock still ticked. I felt for my heart and knew it was still beating. I needed to know if this was real.

"Can you – can you sit down?" I asked. Testing the situation.

"I can."

"Do it, then."

And she did. Even in her phantom transparency, she could sit down in the beanbag chair on the opposite side of the fireplace – the chair she'd always chosen.

I sat across from her on the edge of my bed. The seat I'd always ended up with.

"You don't believe this is real," she observed, reading my posture, my eyes.

"I don't," I said. I couldn't.

"Why do you doubt your senses?"

Because you're dead, I thought.

At this, Marly's ghost raised a frightful noise – half a cry, half a dark laugh. She shook the chain with such a terrifying noise that I had to struggle to stay on the bed. Then, slowly, she unwrapped the scarf from her head. I, who had seen her without hair, who had seen the tumor growing in the X-rays, now had to shut my eyes. I felt myself fall to a kneel.

"Why is this happening?" I cried.

"Look at me, Ben," Marly said gently. I opened my eyes and saw that some of her hair had grown back. Not all of it, not to any length. But a baby-chick fuzz. Almost newborn.

"Do you believe in me or not?" she asked.

"I do," I said. "I always have. I must. But what's going on? What are you now?"

"A spirit. A ghost."

She said this as if it were natural. As if it made perfect sense.

"And why are you here?" I had to know.

"Because I am still tied to this life. Just as you have been tied to this death. As long as the ties are there, I wander through the world and witness what you will not share. While you're caught, I'm caught, Ben. In the in-between."

I looked at her strange chain.

"Don't you recognize it?" she asked. "It's our chain. It was an almost perfect length once. But you have labored on it since. You've made it so heavy. As hard as it will be, you have to stop now. It is a ponderous chain."

I looked down, as if I would suddenly see my own attachment to it. But I couldn't see anything.

"Marly," I implored, "tell me what's happening. Tell me it's going to be okay."

"I can't, Ben – it's not up to me. A very little more is all that is permitted. I cannot rest. I cannot stay. I cannot linger anywhere. Not until you choose."

It was too much. It was too much to have her here and not have it really be her. To see her in this in-between state, to be teetering so violently between found and lost. I felt the truth rise up in me. The real truth. I had to tell her.

"I want to die, Marly," I sobbed. "I want to die without you here."

On hearing this, she set up another cry, this one without any trace of laughter. She clanked the chain so hideously in the dead silence of the night that I was surprised the trees outside did not fall away in fear.

"No, Ben. No. No space or regret can make amends for misusing your life's opportunities," she said fiercely. The stiffer her language, the more a spirit she appeared. "Giving up on love is the same thing as giving up on life itself."

"But aren't you angry, Marly? Aren't you angry that you're not here?"

"That's my point, Ben – you're just not seeing it. On a night like tonight, I suffer the most from looking at you. From seeing what I see."

I didn't know what she meant. I tried to listen, to figure it out, but instead I quivered. With a joy in seeing her, yes. And with a fear of her leaving again.

"Listen to me!" she implored. "My time is nearly gone."

"I will," I promised, trying to get her to stay longer. Forever. "But don't be so hard on me. Tell me what you mean. Why are you here?"

She seemed to be drifting farther and farther off. "How it is that I appear before you in a shape that you can see, I'm not allowed to tell. I have sat invisible beside you many and many a day."

She had been here. It wasn't just my imagination.

"Stay!" I pleaded.

But she shook her head. "There is no light part of what I'm trying to do," she said sadly. "I am here tonight to warn you that you have a chance and hope of escaping your fate. A chance and hope that I've had to work *very* hard to get for you."

Even now, she loved me. I was sure she had found some way for us to be together. For me to be able to put aside this life and step into her continuation.

"You will be haunted by three Spirits," she said.

I gaped at her.

"Is *that* my chance and hope?" I demanded in a faltering voice.

She nodded. "It is."

"I – I think I'd rather not." One spirit was difficult enough.

"Without their visits," Marly said carefully, "you cannot hope to escape the chain. Expect the first when the bell tolls one."

"Couldn't I just take them all at once and have it over with?" I asked, trying to get her back with a joke, to remind her of the way we used to talk.

Marly just went on, making me remember she wasn't entirely Marly anymore. "Expect the second on the next night at the same hour. The third, upon the next night when the last stroke of twelve has ceased to vibrate. Look to see me no more. I have to go. But please, Ben – remember, for your own sake, what has passed between us."

I wanted to tell her I already spent all my time remembering what had passed between us. I was trying to hold on to it all, even as I felt days and minutes and moments slipping away from me. But then I realized she meant tonight. Everything that had passed between us tonight.

Now finished, Marly took her scarf from the table and bound it around her head as before. I reached out for her then, hoping somehow to hold her into staying.

But she walked backwards, away from me. At every step she took, the window raised itself a little, so that it was open when she reached it. She gestured for me to approach then, but when I was two steps away, she held up her hand and warned me not to come nearer. I looked into her eyes and tried to find the part that was unchanged. And there it was – a glimmer of sadness, of longing, of pleading, of regret. The feeling of letting me go.

I stopped – not because I wanted to, but out of surprise and fear. As soon as she'd raised her hand I'd become aware of confused noises in the air, incoherent sounds of lamentation and regret, wailings inexpressibly sorrowful and self-accusatory. Marly's ghost, after listening for a moment, began her own sad love song – pieces of every love song we had ever known, sung as a dirge. Then she floated out upon the bleak, dark night.

I jumped to the window, desperate to keep her, desperate to hear a goodbye. I looked out and gasped in fright.

The air was full of phantoms wandering restlessly,

moaning and singing and sighing as they went. Each one of them wore a chain that led to a house, in town or beyond the horizon.

I saw the man who used to live next door, whose widow now spent all of her time tending his garden, talking to the seeds and the shoots. I saw the girl from our town who had gone missing five years ago, and who now walked through the streets as if frozen in time, her clothes the same as the ones in all of the weather-beaten posters that still emerged from the bottom of crowded bulletin boards. I saw a baby in a tree, watching over a house I didn't know. Every drifting person seemed to be looking for loved ones through a crowd, wanting to interfere, but having lost the power forever.

Whether these phantoms faded into mist or the mist enshrouded them, I couldn't tell. But they and their spirit voices faded together, and the night became as it had been when I'd walked home.

I closed the window and looked at the door Marly had come through. It hadn't been opened. I looked at the beanbag chair. She'd left no imprint. I wanted to dismiss it all, but I couldn't ignore any of it. I was tired from all the feelings that had been forced on me, all the words that had sunk within me one by one. I needed sleep.

Say something, I implored the Marly in my mind. I tried to imagine her responses:

That was so freaky – sorry to interrupt like that. Next time I'll call ahead.

Ben, it was good to see you.

Ben, I'll be back.

Ben, I'm so scared.

But it was just me, pretending to be her.

I had to believe it would be better in the morning.

Without even taking off my shoes, I crawled onto my bed, called out her name helplessly, and fell instantly asleep.

STAVE II
THE FIRST OF
THE THREE SPIRITS

WHEN I WOKE UP, IT WAS SO DARK THAT, LOOKING OUT OF BED, I COULD BARELY TELL THE DIFFERENCE BETWEEN THE WINDOW AND THE WALLS. I was trying to make some sense of the darkness when the chimes of the town church struck four times, marking a new hour. I then waited to count the bells that would come after, to see which hour it was.

I was amazed when the heavy toll went on from six to seven, and from seven to eight, and regularly up to twelve, then stopped. I looked to the clock next to my bed for confirmation. Twelve! It made no sense; I had gone to bed at about two in the morning.

"It isn't possible," I said to myself. I couldn't have slept through a whole day and so far into another night. Maybe the darkness was just a trick of the light. Maybe it was really daytime, and the twelve bells meant it was noon. Maybe the darkness had taken over completely, and all daylight had been eclipsed.

I scrambled out of bed and groped my way to the window. It was so covered with frost that I had to rub it off with my sleeve – and even then I couldn't see very much. All I could make out was that it was still very foggy and extremely cold. There was no sign of life outside, no sign of traffic or walking like there normally would have been at noon. And certainly there wasn't the panic that would have come if night had eclipsed day and taken possession of the world. Even though it seemed ridiculous, I was relieved by that.

I went to bed again and thought . . . and thought . . . and thought it over, and still couldn't figure anything out. The more I thought, the more perplexed I was, and the more I tried not to think, the more I thought.

I couldn't release myself from Marly's ghost. Every time I came close to convincing myself that it had been a dream, my mind flew back again, like a strong spirit released, to what my deepest heart knew was true.

She had been here.

With me.

I couldn't stop wondering what it meant. It wasn't until the clock read 12:45 that I remembered her ghost had said that I'd receive a visitation at one. I resolved to stay awake until the hour had passed; considering I was about as likely to go to sleep as I was to have followed Marly through the window, this wasn't too hard.

The next fifteen minutes were so long that more than once I convinced myself that I had fallen back asleep and missed the chime. But then it came through the air.

Ding-dong!

"A quarter past," I said.

Ding-dong!

"Half past."

Ding-dong!

"Three-quarters past."

I turned to stare at my clock until finally it read:

1:00.

I pulled the sheet over my head, forgetting that my clock was a little fast. I had just closed my eyes when the church bell sounded with a deep, dull, melancholy *one*. I opened my eyes and saw the lights of my room glaring through the sheet.

Before I could think, the sheet was being pulled away from me by a hand I could not yet see. At first all I could take in was the brightness of the room, the glare.

Then I saw a face. Right in front of me. Not even a hand's length away.

It was a girl. A young girl who also looked very old. It was like I was viewing her through some strange lens that gave her the appearance of being far away, diminished to the size of a child. Her hair, which hung around her neck and down her back, was pale, pale blond. Her face didn't have a single wrinkle in it, and her skin bloomed. Her arms were more muscular than a little girl's arms usually are, with hands to match. Her legs and feet, both delicate, were bare. She wore a pure white tunic, and a trophy-colored belt around her waist. She held a bare February branch in her hand and, as if to contradict the branch, her dress was trimmed with summer flowers.

From the crown of her head sprung a bright, clear jet of light, which was making everything visible. Under one arm she held a hat, a floppy cloth winter hat with a small pom-pom on the end.

As I watched, too surprised to scream, her appearance grew even stranger. For as her belt sparkled and glittered from light to dark, her figure itself fluctuated from vague to distinct. Her hair got longer and then shorter. She was wearing overalls, then a Sunday dress – a nightgown – a yellow plastic raincoat. She was a hundred memories all played at once, dissolving and forming and overlapping and melting away. She was a blur of life, and then she stopped. She returned to the form in which she had first greeted me, distinct and near as ever.

I tried to convince myself once again that I was asleep. I tried to convince myself that it wasn't happening. But I failed, and I failed.

"Are you the Spirit that Marly told me about?" I asked, amazed I could even form the question.

"I am," she announced in a soft and gentle voice. It was almost like an echo.

"Who – and what – are you?"

"I am the Ghost of Love Past."

Something about the distance in her voice made me ask, "Of long past?"

"No. *Your* past."

It was too much for me. Especially the light, the brightness. I had grown so used to the comfort of the dark. I begged the Spirit to cover her head with her cap.

"What!" she exclaimed. "Would you so soon put out, with worldly hands, the light I give? Haven't you been making me wear the cap for long enough? Are you really so afraid of the brightness?"

"I'm sorry," I said, bewildered. "I had no idea. Whatever I did, I didn't mean to. But I need to know – I have to know – why are you here?"

"Your welfare!" the Ghost replied in a singsong voice.

"Thank you for that," I said, trying to be polite, while thinking: *All I want is to go back to sleep. Easy oblivion. Nothing. Please give me that nothing again.*

But the Ghost wasn't going to let me return there.

"Your reclamation, then," she said. "Take heed!"

She put out her strong hand as she spoke and clasped me gently by the arm.

"Rise, and walk with me!" she commanded, like a child who knew exactly what to do.

There was no use in arguing. I could've said that I wanted to go to sleep, that it was too cold out, that I wasn't dressed to go anywhere, that I wasn't feeling well. I could've said, *This is completely absurd.* But those were only words, unconnected to me and the Spirit. Her grasp, though gentle as a little girl's, was not to be resisted. I rose from my bed, ready to follow. But then I saw she was steering me toward the window . . . with the full intention of jumping out.

"Wait a second!" I protested. "I can't just jump out of a window!"

"Bear but a touch of my hand *there*," the Spirit said, laying her hand upon my heart, "and you shall be upheld in more than this!"

As she said this, we passed through the wall. Instead

49

of falling to the ground below, I found myself on different ground altogether. I wasn't outside my house anymore. It had entirely vanished . . . along with the darkness and the mist. It was now a clear, cold winter day, with snow upon the ground.

"Whoa," I said, clasping my hands together as I looked around, totally freaked out. "This is my elementary school."

And indeed it was, down to the valentine decorations taped up haphazardly in the windows.

The Spirit gazed upon me mildly. Her gentle touch, though it had been light and instantaneous, was still with me. I was conscious of a thousand childhood odors floating in the air. Cookies just out of the oven and Elmer's glue. My mother's evening perfume and a freshly opened box of crayons. The newsprint of shared comic books. The slightly rancid odor of the pinnies we had to wear for gym. The comforting smell of Fred's house when I went to visit. The smell of bubbles blown in chocolate milk.

"Your lip is trembling," observed the Ghost. "And what is that upon your cheek?"

Much to my surprise, it was a tear. But I wasn't ready to admit this. So I pretended she was talking about something else on my cheek, and said it was a pimple.

She didn't comment on that. "You recollect the way?" she inquired.

"Of course," I told her. "I could walk it blindfolded."

"Strange to have forgotten it before," the Ghost observed. "Let us go on."

As we walked up the driveway, I recognized every gate and post and tree. Every rung of the ladder leading up to the slide, every turn around every base of the playing field. Suddenly the school bell rang and a mob of cheering children came running outside, decked in colorful hats and snow jackets. Everyone was so happy, shouting to one another until the playground and field were so full of music that the crisp air laughed to hear it.

"These are but shadows of the things that have been," said the Ghost. "They have no consciousness of us."

The kids came rushing forward, forming

constellations over the jungle gyms and dotting the snow with boot-sized prints – a reverse Braille that spelled out happiness. I knew each and every one of them: Cat . . . Donna . . . Justin Number One . . . Fred . . . Davey . . . Sheila . . . Andrew . . . Justin Number Two . . . Eddie . . . Jenny . . . Justin Number Three . . .

Seeing them filled me with a feeling that was almost like rejoicing. It wasn't just the sight of Justin Number Two falling to the ground to make an impromptu snow angel, or Sheila and Davey playing run-catch-and-kiss around the basketball pole. Or even the fact that when they unzipped their jackets, there was almost always something red underneath. No, it wasn't what they were doing, or the gleeful innocence of it all. It was the familiarity that got to me. The connection I felt then, and was feeling now. It had been a long time since I'd felt so connected to the past.

She was the only piece missing. She was the one I was looking for. But I couldn't find her, and it was only after stopping to think that I realized why: This was second grade, maybe third. She was still living in another town, another state. Her feet had yet to touch this ground.

"The school is not quite deserted," the Ghost said, interrupting my thoughts. "A solitary child is left there still."

We walked to the school. I could feel the snow below my bare feet, but I left no imprint. When we got to the door, it was as if I hadn't grown since third grade. Even though I knew I was taller, the doors still seemed impossibly big. I expected the Spirit to grab hold again and pull me through, but instead she waited until I pushed open the door and entered the hall. The linoleum was as polished as ever. The display outside the library was full of picture books about love. My classroom was exactly where I'd left it.

It was quiet here at recess, all the joy noises coming from outside. Inside there was the sound of the heater rattling like it had snakes coiled within, steadily hissing heat. The desks were arranged in the usual rows, pencils and papers sitting where they'd been dropped when the recess bell rang.

The room was empty, except for me.

There I was, at the desk between Susan's (on the left)

and Fred's (on the right). There I was, decorating my valentine shoebox, preparing for the valentine delivery that afternoon.

The Spirit touched me on the arm and pointed to my younger self, who was so intent upon his feats of decoration.

I remembered that box. The Reebok logo covered over by layer upon layer of tin foil. The hole scissored in the top, for the store-bought and homemade cards to be slipped inside. My own cards were by my elbow, sealed in their nearly transparent white envelopes, awaiting their tense distribution. Some were signed *Love*, some were signed *Your friend*, and the rest were just signed with my initials.

It's not that I'd waited until the last minute. Both of my parents had helped me cut and glue and smooth out the tin. But I didn't feel it was complete. It didn't say everything I wanted my valentine shoebox to say. So I was staying in at recess, pasting on pictures I'd drawn of the things that had popped into my head – a green parrot, a Sultan's Groom turned upside down by the magical Ali-Baba, a vaguely-featured princess.

I had an intense frown of concentration on my face as I chose which picture would go where. Then, when it was all done, I broke into a relieved smile. Other kids had decorated their boxes with cartoon characters or simple valentine hearts. That hadn't been enough for me.

"There's the parrot!" I said to the Spirit, admiring my own handiwork. "Green body and yellow tail, with a thing like a lettuce growing out of the top of his head. It's just the way I remember it."

It made me wish, for a brief second, that I'd done something for this Valentine's Day. Not for myself – I felt so beyond that. But for this younger version of me. Because right now it felt that without such things, this younger version of me was dead.

"I wish . . ." I muttered. Then I caught myself and said, "But it's too late now."

"What is the matter?" the Spirit asked plaintively.

"Nothing," I replied. And even though it was meant as an evasion, it was also the truth: The nothingness was the matter.

The Ghost smiled thoughtfully and waved her hand.

Then she said, "Look."

We were in a different classroom, a couple of doors down. And I was different, a couple of years older. In the same spot in the classroom, at the desk next to Fred's. He was there now with me, jostling my elbow as I tried to draw a caricature of Dr. O'Desky, our fifth-grade teacher.

I jostled Fred back and didn't notice when Dr. O'Desky walked into the room with a shy blond girl at her side.

I wasn't looking the moment that Marly first walked into my life. Now, older, I could barely breathe. I felt chills and warmth and tears and gladness. Only the Spirit's presence next to me was calm. This was it, the very, very start of it, unfolding in front of my eyes. One of the memories – the very first memory – that I had lost.

I looked at her as she teetered from foot to foot in a dress that was slightly too new, slightly too nice. And I didn't look at her, still sitting at the desk and drawing away. It wasn't until Dr. O'Desky cleared her throat that the younger me looked up. First at Dr. O'Desky . . . and then at the girl. Putting the pencil down, leaving the drawing unfinished, as Dr. O'Desky announced that we had someone new to our school, whose name was Marly. I didn't pick the pencil back up; I didn't write down this new, strange name or have any idea how it would eventually become so intertwined with my own. No, I just looked at her and scooted my desk a little bit aside when she walked past me in the aisle. I didn't notice how vulnerable she was, how nervous.

Witnessing this, I was so shot through with thoughts

that I couldn't do a thing. If I had actually been in the past, if I could have leaned over and told my younger self everything that was going to happen – would I have warned him? Would I have stopped it for all the hurt that was going to come?

No. I would've let it happen.

I turned to the Spirit, but she didn't give anything away.

"Always a delicate creature, whom a breath might have withered," she said. "But she had a large heart!"

I agreed. That nervousness never fully went away, nor the vulnerability. But she had such a heart.

I closed my eyes, remembering our eighth-grade dance. As we box-stepped, as I left my hands on her nearly non-existent hips and reveled in the fact that I had a girlfriend, she was telling me that I really had to ask Julie Pearl to dance once, because otherwise Julie was going to sit on the bleachers the whole night, looking sad. So I asked Julie to dance for the next song, and kept stealing glances of Marly, who hung awkwardly on the side, smiling every time Julie and I shifted so I was facing her. That night, my father drove us home. I walked Marly to her door, out of sight of my father's car in the driveway. We hovered for a second before she rang the doorbell. She'd had a good time. I said I'd had a good time. We teetered. And then, for a moment so quick I might have missed it, we both leaned in and touched our lips into a soft, sudden kiss. It was over before I could worry about what to do. She rang the doorbell and her mother was at the door in an instant. Marly said goodbye, and I was still in such surprised happiness that I stood there for another minute after the door was closed, absorbing it all.

I remembered her leaving through that front door. Then I opened my eyes and found that the Spirit and I were in front of a certain warehouse door.

"Know it?" the Spirit asked.

"Know it!" I exclaimed. "This is where I learned everything."

It couldn't be anywhere else – we had to be at Fezziwig's.

Fezziwig had been a senior when I was a freshman. It was only dumb luck that had brought me into his orbit – during our first week of school, he had put flyers for a Creative Anachronism Club into a dozen randomly selected lockers. I had gotten one, and was the only kid to show up at the "orientation." Fezziwig was a big guy – if he'd been two inches taller, he would have knocked his head on most ceilings – but he filled every inch of his soul with what I can only call mirth.

His parents were artists, and every now and then they'd let Fezziwig throw a party in their studio. This was where the Spirit and I now stood.

"Why, it's Fezziwig!" I cried in great excitement as we walked inside. "He's back!"

Sure enough, the Fezziwig I remembered was sitting at his high desk, scribbling away in one of the ledgers he used as notebooks. Then he laid down his pen and looked up at the clock. I knew exactly what occasion this was: Valentine's Day three years ago. I knew this because of Fezziwig's outfit – a capacious waistcoat and a cupid-print tie. Rubbing his hands, he called out in a comfortable, jovial voice:

"Yo ho, there! Ben! Marly!"

My former self came in briskly from another room, accompanied by fourteen-year-old Marly. We were both used to the way Fezziwig talked – this wonderful affectation that was so ridiculous that it couldn't possibly be considered pretentious.

"Yo ho, my boys!" said Fezziwig. "We're having a party to end all parties, so let's have the shutters up before a man can say Jack Robinson!"

I rarely knew what he was talking about, but it didn't matter – if I didn't know the specific phrasings, I knew the enthusiasm that lay underneath. It was amazing how quickly Marly and I went to work, charging to the windows and opening all of the shutters before you could count to twelve, panting like racehorses when the effort was through.

"Hilli-ho!" cried Fezzwig, skipping down from the high desk with amazing agility for a guy his size. "Clear away, my lads, and let's have lots of room here! Hilli-ho, Marly! Chirrup, Ben!"

Clear away! There was nothing we wouldn't have cleared away, or couldn't have cleared away, with Fezziwig looking on. Fezziwig loved to be larger than life, and Marly and I were happy apprentices to that. After being together in a big way for more than a year, we were still astonished to find ourselves sharing so much together. I think Fezziwig enjoyed our glow as much as we enjoyed his. When we'd been apart, Marly and I had each felt like halves. But together, we were so much more than that.

We cleared the warehouse in what seemed like a minute. Every movable object was packed off for its own safety; the floor was swept and shined, the colored lightbulbs were fitted into their sockets, and fuel was heaped upon the fire, our best source of heat. The warehouse was as snug and warm and dry and bright a ballroom as you would hope to see on a winter's night. It was something magical.

In came a DJ with his milk crates of records. He went up to the lofty desk and made a DJ booth out of it, preparing his backbeats as Marly, Fezziwig, and I put out bowls of candy and bigger bowls of love-red punch. Fezziwig's mother poked her head in, showing one vast, substantial smile, followed by his beaming and lovable father and curious little sister.

In no time, the guests began to swirl in, throwing their jackets onto easels, revealing the soul of their clothes. In they came, one after another – some shyly, some boldly; some gracefully, some awkwardly; some pushing, some pulling – anyhow and everyhow, as Fezziwig would say. It was a conversational and flirtatious dance, couples and singles all at once, hands fluttering and faces tilted in laughter, friends walking to one corner, then through the middle to another corner to greet another group. Old couples running into each other in the wrong place; new couples starting off on their newfound footing. The air was filled with the music of a dozen or more conversations, with the DJ's loops and snares moving underneath.

I had found an old orchestra conductor's jacket in a thrift store a few days before, and was wearing it as the DJ pushed the music harder and I bopped and flailed and burned along. Marly was wearing a dress the color of cinnamon, chosen to match the shoes I'd just bought her, the ones she'd wanted so badly. For the fast songs, we danced without touching, opening ourselves out into circles upon circles of friends and strangers. For the slow songs, she lifted her hands behind my neck so I could feel the charms of her bracelet lightly against my skin. I knew then how happy I felt, but it wasn't until now, watching, that I witnessed how happy I looked. Every joy I saw in her was reflected in me.

At one point, Fezziwig clapped his hands to stop the dancing, crying out, "Well done!" The DJ plunged his hot face into a pot of punch, especially provided for that purpose. Upon his reappearance he instantly began again. He moved as if a first DJ had been carried home, exhausted, and he was a brand-new man resolved to beat him out of sight.

There were more dances, and there were forfeits and more dances, and there was cake, and there was a game we called Cupid's Arrow, and there were pies and plenty of punch. But the best part of the evening came after the cake, when the artful DJ struck up the Sir Roger de Coverley remix of a Madonna song. Then Fezziwig stood out to dance with Marly, and I was happy to oblige. Soon they were surrounded on the floor by other dancers who were not to be trifled with, people who *would* dance, even if it meant they wouldn't be able to walk after.

But if there had been twice as many people on the warehouse floor – or even four times as many – Fezziwig and Marly would have been a match for them. She was worthy to be his partner, and I lavished her with high praise from the sidelines, happy to see her throw her hesitations to the floor and be happy. A positive light appeared to issue from her, shining in every part of the dance like moonlight. As if rehearsed, she and Fezziwig took over the floor with some old-style moves. And when they had gone all through the dance – advance and retire, both hands to your partner, bow and curtsey, corkscrew, thread-the-needle and back again to your place – Fezziwig cut so deftly that he appeared to wink with his legs, coming up on his feet again without a stagger.

The whole crowd burst into applause. Even the unpresent I, standing next to the Spirit, silently applauded.

When the clock struck eleven, the dance broke up. Fezziwig took his station by the door, shaking hands with the guests as they went out, wishing them love.

Marly found me again and said she was feeling a

little woozy. I assured her it was just the dancing, and she easily agreed.

We were the last ones to shake Fezziwig's hand and wish him a good night. I watched as the two of us left the room. My heart and soul were in the scene. I corroborated everything, remembered everything, enjoyed everything. It wasn't until now, when the bright faces of my former self and Marly had turned from me and the Spirit, that I remembered the Ghost and became conscious that she was looking fully at me. The light upon her head burned very clear.

"Such a small thing," she said, "to make these folks so full of gratitude."

"Small!" I echoed incredulously.

"It's just a party," the Spirit pointed out.

"It isn't that," I said. "You have to understand – he's one of those people who find the greatest happiness in making everyone else happy. He didn't have to do it; he could have used his wit to taunt us just as easily as he used it to embrace us. His power came from words and looks, from things so slight and insignificant that it's impossible to count them. The happiness he gave us was priceless. It was *never* just a party."

I watched as Fezziwig began to clear the remnants of the celebration, then smiled to himself and gave up for the night. It was only then that I let myself step out of the moment. Even though I couldn't see my younger self and Marly anymore, I knew where they were going. We had planned such a big night – she had told her parents she was staying at Sarah's, and I had told my parents that I was staying at Fred's. But instead Fezziwig had given us the key to his place, a small apartment above his family's garage. It was going to be our first night alone together. I had brought champagne and strawberries. She had carefully selected the music.

But of course when we got there, her wooziness hadn't gone away. I carved little valentine hearts into the Tylenol before she took them.

It didn't help.

Nothing would end up helping . . . although we didn't know it then. So we could still eat strawberries and play music quietly and leave the champagne for another day and kiss slow-gently and sleep a whole night in the same bed, each of us waking constantly, muttering contentments before going back to sleep.

My heart had grown too warm to freeze again immediately. So as I stood there in the dark warehouse, I was everything in-between. The full range of feeling.

"My time grows short," observed the Spirit. "Quick!"

This was not addressed to me, or to anyone I could see, but it produced an immediate effect. Once again I saw myself. I was almost two years older now. My face didn't have the harsh and rigid grief lines that were soon to come, but it had begun to show the signs of care and concern. There was an eager, despairing, restless motion in my eye, which showed the passion that had taken root, and where the shadow of the growing tree would fall.

I was not alone, but sat by Marly's side on the bench we always snuck out to, in the park a few blocks from her house. There were tears in her eyes, which brightened in the light that shone out of the Ghost of Love Past.

"It doesn't matter," Marly said softly. "Please don't."

The treatments had begun, and her hair had fallen out. She refused to wear a wig, and instead braved the world baldly, beautifully.

"I want to," I said.

I remembered this argument so well. When her hair had started falling out, I cut mine shorter and shorter. Now I wanted to shave it off completely. So she wouldn't be alone.

"Don't," she said again, this time a little angrier.

I tried to joke. "We'll be like one of those couples who wear matching outfits, only we'll polish each other's heads."

"Stop – "

"Why? We can even get matching scarves if you want."

She wasn't laughing. "You don't get it, do you?"

"Get what?" I asked, a little irritated now that my selfless gesture was being turned away.

"That I'm not *choosing* this. That I love your hair. That it's bad enough for me to be like this. But to have you like this – to not be able to reach over and run my fingers through your hair – there's no reason for that. I don't want anything else taken away."

"But Marly – "

"No."

"I'd like – "

"*Stop it*. There's no use. Don't you understand that? *There's no use*."

It was the first time she'd said it. Or maybe just the first time I'd heard it. She cried more. I held her tighter.

"Don't say that," I pleaded. "Don't give up."

Her hand grasped my sweater. "Everything's changed. Can't you see that?"

"My feelings haven't changed."

She shook her head.

"You think they have?" I asked, afraid.

She wouldn't look at me.

"We've been together a long time," she said. "But we fell in love when we were both . . . okay. When love wasn't so complicated. Now it's very, very complicated. You know it is."

"But I still love you as much as I ever did. More."

"We're not the same. All the things we were looking forward to at the start – they're just going to haunt us more if we don't get there. If we're apart. I can't tell you how much I've thought about this, Ben. But it's the right thing to do. I can release you. I have to."

This was incomprehensible to me. "Have I ever asked to be *released*?" I said.

"In words? No. Never."

"In what, then?"

"You would never say it. But sometimes I can see it in your eyes. Or hear it in your voice – there's something there that wants to go in another direction. And I can't blame you. Tell me – would you ask me out now? Like this?"

Not believing her doubt in me, I said, with a struggle, "You think I wouldn't."

"I would be happy to think otherwise, if I could," she answered. "I know how strong and irresistible it is to think that everything can be so solid. But if you were free today, tomorrow, yesterday, would you really choose to go out with a sick girl – a *dying* girl? You, Ben, who are always thinking in terms of life and love and the future? And even if you can believe that you would choose me, I'm sure you'll regret it. So I release you. Honestly. You deserve better than this."

"I can't believe you're saying this."

It's not that I hadn't made choices. Every day I made choices. I found the strength to see her, to cheer her, to not look away. It was taking a toll, but it was a toll I willingly paid. I hadn't questioned it, because I believed she never questioned it either.

"It's okay," she said.

I took hold of her chin and moved her eyes so they matched mine. "No, it's not okay," I insisted. "Stop it. I'm not leaving you. Ever. And you can't give up. You're going to beat this. *We're* going to beat this."

"But what if we don't? I don't want you cutting your hair off for me. I don't want you ripping your heart up for me. Do you understand that? It's not going to get better, Ben. It's going to get much, much worse. And then maybe after that it will get better again. *Maybe*."

"It will."

"You don't know that."

"And you don't know otherwise. You're too young to –"

"What? Die?"

"No. To *know*. You're too young to know. We can't give up. Promise me you won't give up."

She shook her head slightly. "I can't."

I pulled away a little then. Recoiling even from the thought. "What do you mean?"

"I don't want to promise it. Because what happens if I can't keep the promise?"

"You will. Please. Promise me."

"But I'm letting you go."

"I'm not leaving."

"I can't."

"Please."

And then she began to shake. That horrible shaking, like a fragile marionette under the hand of a cruel and violent child.

"Spirit!" I cried. "I don't want to see any more. Take me home. Do you *enjoy* torturing me?"

Because I knew she had never promised. No matter how hard I tried. And the whole time I thought I was asking her not to give up on life. But I was also begging her not to give up on us. On me.

"One shadow more!" exclaimed the Ghost.

"No more!" I pleaded. I knew where the story would go. "I don't want to see it. Stop!"

But the relentless ghost pinioned me and forced me to observe what happened next.

We were in another scene and place – a room, not very large or handsome, but full of attempted comfort. Marly's room. Such a mix of things on the walls: boy-band posters from when she was little, which she now loved for their pure cheesiness; shelves of books, from well-worn copies of *Goodnight Moon* and *Snowy Day* to unopened paperbacks by Ayn Rand and Nabokov; and photographs she'd taken of me over the years, from the awkward class trip snapshots – me with the hippo from the zoo, me mimicking the torch-holding of the Statue of Liberty – to the more recent pictures of me sleeping in her bed, the afternoon light washing over my naked shoulders. I knew the room almost as if it was my own; I saw my books on the shelves, my CDs scattered around the stereo. I had lived here, once. Not daily, but hourly. It was more home to me than home.

Now I looked to the bed, and knew the point we'd come to.

We were near the end.

I was by the side of her bed, holding her hand. Her breathing was shallow, a seashore slowly being covered with water. Her words had gained an urgency. She knew it was near the end.

"I had this dream," she said, her voice so soft I would've missed it if I hadn't already been leaning so close. "Only it wasn't a dream. I was awake, thinking. And I could see what I was thinking. I could picture it. I was this beautiful woman, and I was in this room full of children. There was a girl there too. She looked like us. There was so much noise and everyone was laughing. The kids were playing a game. I wanted so much to be playing with them. Crawling around, knocking things over. And laughing. The young girl – she was so pretty. Everything about her – her tiny shoes, her lips, her hair – was so precious.

"Then there was a knock on the door and everyone rushed toward it. It was you at the door, Ben, and you had a big stupid grin on your face and a big heart-shaped box of chocolates under your arm. You were older, but I would've recognized you anywhere. The kids were all over you – they loved you so much – climbing on you to dive into your pockets, to hug you around the neck. You opened the box of chocolates and inside there were a dozen smaller boxes, which you handed out to each and every one of them. You made them so happy. Then you handed me the big box, and I thought it would be empty, but somehow it was full again. It was full of roses and poems and candy kisses. Then one of the kids said the baby had put a doll's frying pan into his mouth, and perhaps a plastic valentine heart as well. It was a false alarm, and we were both so relieved when we saw the baby was okay. So joyful, so grateful."

Marly paused, and I gave her some water, knowing her needs before she needed to say them. After she'd swallowed, after I'd put the glass back down, she continued.

"The kids went away with their presents, leaving one by one to their rooms upstairs. All but the girl, who sat down with the two of us by the fireplace – like the one in your room. I was happy then. So happy. Not just in the dream, but as I was seeing the dream.

"Then you turned to me, our daughter on your lap, and you said, a little sadly, 'I was thinking of someone today.'

"And I asked, 'Who was it?'

"You asked me to guess. And I said, 'How can I?' Then I thought about it, remembering it was Valentine's Day."

Marly paused for another moment, closed her eyes to concentrate, then opened them and went on.

"All of a sudden it struck me. You were thinking of me. And I wasn't myself anymore. This whole scene – I'd been seeing it through the eyes of another woman – your wife. Someone else.

"So I said – and this wasn't easy – 'You were thinking of Marly.'

"And you said, 'Yes, I was.'

"And I understood, Ben. I understood."

Speaking for so long exhausted her. I was crying now. She had run out of tears. But the sickness hadn't taken the care out of her voice.

"I know this is going to hurt you," she said. "And I have to admit that I'd rather you be hurt than feel nothing. What I mean is – I want you to remember me. I do. But I don't want you to give up. Please. Don't give up."

And I promised I wouldn't. Right there in the dying light of that afternoon, I held her hand and kissed her forehead and promised I wouldn't give up. And at the same time I knew that something inside of me was dying too. Irrevocably.

Her energy was now gone; she could no longer speak. Since I had witnessed her decline gradually, the true horror of her state never fully struck me until the very end. Now, standing apart from the scene, it did all over again. As the two of us – my past self, my present self – hovered over her bed, I could see each cruel damage written across her skin, beneath her eyes, down into her bones. She was no longer the way she wanted to be remembered. She was already more breath than body.

"Spirit," I whispered in a broken voice, "take me away from this place."

"I told you these were shadows of things that have been," she said. "That they are what they are, do not blame me."

"Get me out of here!" I screamed, turning away from Marly, from myself, from this memory. "I can't do this!"

I turned on the Ghost, and she looked at me with a face that, in some strange way, contained fragments of all the faces she had shown me. The hopes, the expectations, the breakage, the pain.

"Leave me!" I said. "Take me back. Don't haunt me anymore."

I grabbed hold of her with the same force with which she had grabbed me. I wanted to wrestle myself out of this room, out of the past. The Ghost, with no visible resistance on her part, was undisturbed by my effort. Her light was still burning high and bright. I couldn't stand it any longer. I seized the cap out of her hand and pressed it down on her head.

The Spirit dropped beneath it, so the hat covered her whole body. But even as I pressed with all my force, I could not hide the light. It streamed from under the rim, an unbroken flood upon the ground.

I was conscious of being exhausted, and overcome by an irresistible drowsiness. Realizing I was back in my bedroom, I gave the cap a parting squeeze, and then my hand relaxed. I had barely time to reel to bed before I sank into a heavy sleep.

STAVE III

THE SECOND OF
THE THREE SPIRITS

AWAKING IN THE MIDDLE OF A SNORE, AND SITTING UP IN BED TO GET MY THOUGHTS TOGETHER, I KNEW IMMEDIATELY THAT THE BELL WAS AGAIN UPON THE STROKE OF ONE. I felt I'd been restored to consciousness right in the nick of time, ready to encounter Marly's second messenger.

Well, not exactly ready. A chill seized me when I wondered where the next Spirit would come from. I wouldn't try to hide under the sheets this time. Instead, I kept my eyes wide open. I wanted to challenge the Spirit on the moment of its appearance.

At this point, I felt nothing between a baby and a

rhinoceros would have astonished me much.

Still . . . being prepared for anything didn't prepare me for *nothing*. But nothing is exactly what appeared when the bell outside struck one. No shape came through my door. No Phantom. Five minutes, ten minutes, a quarter of an hour went by . . . yet nothing came. Gradually I realized that my room was not as dark as it should have been . . . that there was, in fact, a growing blaze of light coming from underneath the door. Like the ominous chords in a horror movie soundtrack, this simple, spreading light made me more and more alarmed the more it persisted and amplified. I had no idea what it meant, and felt powerless there in my bed. It made me afraid to move – as if somehow my movement would set it off, and all the light would turn to flame.

I tried to think about it rationally. If I didn't know what the light was, I could at least try to find its source. It wasn't coming from the window or the air itself. Instead, it seemed to be flooding in from the hallway. I knew I wouldn't be able to do anything until I checked it out, so I got off my bed and shuffled toward the door.

The moment my hand was on the doorknob, a strange voice called me by my name and asked me to enter.

I obeyed.

It was my own room. There was no doubt about that. I stood in my room, opened the door, and looked through the doorway into my own room once again. It had undergone a surprising transformation. It was as if every darkness and every shadow had been banished. The colors were now ten times as bright as they had been before, and the objects that had once been black or white were now Technicolor. The walls and ceiling were covered with such a living green that it looked like a grove, from every part of which thumbtacks glistened like berries. The books on my bookshelf wore staccato-rainbow spines, and the jewel cases of my CDs had become jewels in their own right, reflecting back the light as if so many little mirrors had been scattered there. Such a blaze went roaring up the chimney that I barely recognized the sound of my fireplace.

Heaped upon the floor, to form a kind of throne,

were stacks and stacks of letters and envelopes, built like a house of cards. All of the greetings intermingled, the small collaged love affairs beside the Snoopy-gilded messages. There were photos of lovers in Paris, toddler scribbles, computer-composed reveries, four-times-folded notes of friendship, tearful calligraphies of caring. I inhaled the sudden scent of cherry-cheeked apples, juicy oranges, luscious pears, blushing red wine – all the ingredients of love-red punch, making the room breathe with its delicious steam.

On top of the couch of cards there sat an amazing and tall figure holding a glowing torch in the shape of a cornucopia. As I walked through the door, she held the torch up, high up, to shed its light on me.

"Come in!" exclaimed the Ghost. "Come in and know me better!"

I entered timidly, hanging my head before this Spirit. Even though her eyes were clear and kind, I didn't want to meet them. I didn't feel worthy – I didn't feel I had enough kindness left in me to give back to her.

"I am the Ghost of Love Present!" said the Spirit. "Look upon me!"

I did so, reverently. She was clothed in one simple, deep-green robe, bordered with white faux fur. I couldn't tell if she was a woman or a man dressed as a woman. Her feet were bare, and on her head she wore a wreath made of postage stamps. Her dark-brown curls were long and free as her friendly face, her sparkling eyes, her open hand, her cheery voice. Around her waist was an antique scabbard. But there was no sword there, and the ancient sheath was eaten up with rust.

"I'll bet you've never seen the like of me before!" exclaimed the Spirit.

"Never," I agreed, thinking this was quite an understatement.

The Ghost of Love Present rose.

I wasn't going to fight this. If I'd been freaked out by the appearance of the first Ghost, now I felt – not prepared or ready, but resigned, I guess. I was trapped, and the only way out was to go along. As much as I'd hated the ending, I was thankful to the first Spirit for showing me those moments with Marly again. I hoped that this Ghost would bring me back to her too.

"Spirit," I said submissively, "take me wherever you want. Your wish is my command. I learned a lesson last night which is working now. Tonight if you have something to teach me, let me learn from it too."

The Ghost must have been happy with this response, because she stepped forward and said, "Touch my robe!"

I did as I was told, and held it fast.

All the letters and cards disappeared, as did the room and the fire. We stood in the middle of town on Valentine's Day morning, where (for the weather was severe) the people made a rough but brisk kind of music, scraping the snow from the pavement and from the tops of the houses. The neighborhood kids were so excited to see it come plumping down into the road below, splitting into snowstorms as it fell.

The house fronts looked dark enough, and the windows darker, contrasting with the smooth white sheet of snow upon the roofs. The dirtier snow sat upon the ground, which had been plowed up in deep furrows from the street. The sky was gloomy, and the shorter streets were choked up with a dingy mist, half thawed, half frozen, whose heavier particles descended in a shower of sooty atoms, as if all the fireplaces in town had been ignited at once and were blazing away to their hearts' content. There was nothing very cheerful about the cold, and yet there was an air of cheerfulness that the clearest summer air and brightest summer sun couldn't have competed with. Everyone was in this together.

The door of one house opened and a woman came trudging out to deliver something to her husband, who was shoveling the front walk. I recognized a red envelope from what had once been the Spirit's throne.

"Were those all valentines?" I asked her.

"From the ones who mean it," she replied.

The man put down his shovel and took off his gloves to rip open the envelope. The two of them laughed when he had trouble getting the card out. Finally he opened it, and as he read, his face opened too. Without a word, he widened his arms and welcomed her into his overcoat embrace.

"What did it say?" I asked the Ghost.

"That's none of your business," she replied.

The couple glowed in color against the snow. The Ghost led me forward, and I found the glow had spread throughout my quiet town. I saw two girls from my school jovially shouting of their affections from the parapets, then throwing snowballs at each other with spirited glee. Enjoying the childhood of their love, the feeling of being outdoors and free and together.

I recognized that.

Farther down the street, the local greengrocer had banished the vegetables to the back of her store, garlanding the day with the fruitiest bouquets. There were pears and apples, clustered high in blooming pyramids. There were bunches of grapes dangling from conspicuous hooks, so people's mouths might water free of charge as they passed. Before, I would have walked by without noticing any of it. Now I breathed in the piles of filberts, mossy and brown, remembering walks in the woods and ankle-deep shufflings through withered leaves.

As I watched, the greengrocer's three granddaughters came into the store and presented her with their carefully constructed hearts. Even the tiniest girl had signed her name, and the greengrocer showered them in return with absolute delight.

The only interruption to this was a customer – a person I knew well. Fred had three pineapples bundled into his arms; as he paid, he admired the granddaughters' handiwork enthusiastically. The girls giggled and hid their faces shyly in reply.

"Fred!" I said. But he didn't turn or notice.

"He can't hear you," the Ghost reminded me.

We followed as Fred walked two doors down, to the florist.

The florist! In all the weeks leading up to this day, I had forgotten the radiance with which our florist greeted Valentine's Day each year. Marly and I had loved it so much – which was, perhaps, why I had blocked it out. This florist was, I believe, the only florist in the entire country who actually *lowered* his prices when February 14th came around. As a result, the town swarmed to his shop like bees, and the store was a hive of cheer as stems were lifted and petals admired. And what flowers they were! Roses that seemed sewn of velvet, and tulips that defied the calendar to make a fevered appearance. Orchids dropped from the ceiling like bells, while geranium plants watched matronly over the smaller patches of schoolgirl violets. Juniper explosions, cornflowers convening – even the baby's breath seemed to exhale a sweet fragrance as the florist bowed from row to row, composing dazzling mismatched bouquets that always, always worked perfectly together. Marly and I had always lived for such details, and the sharing of them. *Did you see that?* had been our most frequently asked question.

A woman spent what seemed like hours composing the words to fit on the one-inch square of greeting that would accompany her bouquet. She wrote with such flustered determination that I just knew the card was one that had been a part of the Spirit's throne. Fred had already written his card, and tucked it into the rainbow of roses that he'd chosen. Then he took the envelope out, kissed it quickly, and slid it back in. The spot he kissed was where he'd written Sarah's name.

"Come!" the Spirit exclaimed, and suddenly I was

spinning headlong through town, the day unwinding from love letter to love letter. I never saw what words were written, except the invisible ones I could translate from the look of an eye, the depth of a smile, the meaning of a touch. Old couples celebrating their seventieth Valentine's Day. Young couples making the first tentative, nervous steps toward having something they could deem real. Friends passing each other pop-up books made from notebook paper and tape. Mothers and fathers displaying cards like open books across the kitchen table, little libraries of celebration and love.

"It's just because it's Valentine's Day – a commercial, Hallmark-funded holiday," I said.

The Ghost shook her head and clucked her tongue.

"This day isn't special," she said. "We just happen to be on this day. These kinds of things happen all the time, in different ways."

For every couple we saw, I noticed a certain incense pass from the Ghost's torch onto their letters and words. It didn't matter who was in the couple, or what their relationship was. Rich and poor, friend and lover, any race, gay and straight, old and young . . . this very unusual torch graced them all with its magic. Even when fights threatened to break out, the substance would touch down and it was all good again.

"That stuff in your torch – is there a particular flavor to it?" I asked the Spirit.

"There is. My own."

"Would it apply to any kind of person?"

"To any kindly given. To a fearful one most."

"Why to a fearful one most?"

"Because a fearful one needs it most."

The Spirit looked so angelic at that moment. *So religious.* I thought of all the restrictions still put on love – sometimes in the name of love. People who were weighed down with obstacle over obstacle. I couldn't understand. If the Spirit could spread her magic, did that mean she withheld it as well?

"Spirit," I said after a moment of thought, "I hope you don't mind if I ask a question. I don't really know where you're coming from, or who your boss is, exactly. But . . . if you're so generous about love, why do you always make it so hard?"

"I!" cried the Spirit.

"In your presence, people pass judgment about who can and can't love. In your presence, awful things happen that cause love to end. You don't stop that."

"I!"

"You seek to stop some people from loving each other. And it comes to the same thing."

"*I* seek!"

"Forgive me if I am wrong. It has been done in your name, or at least in that of your kind," I said, meaning: *In the name of God. In the name of love.*

"There are some upon this earth of yours," returned the Spirit, "who claim to know us, and who do their deeds of passion, pride, ill will, hatred, envy, bigotry, and selfishness in our name, who are as strange to us, and all our kith and kin, as if they had never lived. Remember that, and charge their doings on themselves, not us."

I promised I would, and we went on, as invisible as we had been before, farther into the suburbia of my town. It was a remarkable quality of the Ghost that, despite her gigantic size, she could make herself fit wherever we went, and that she stood beneath a low roof just as gracefully as she could have done in any lofty hall.

Perhaps it was the pleasure the good Spirit had in showing off this power of hers, or maybe it was her own kind and generous nature and her sympathy with all of humankind that led us to a room I'd never thought I'd see again. It was Fezziwig's old place, the one that Marly and I had escaped to after his Valentine's Day dance. At the threshold of the door, the Spirit, smiling, stopped to bless Fezziwig's dwelling with the sprinklings of her torch.

We were alone in the apartment for merely a minute, enough for me to look at the surroundings – the one simple room, the bed in the corner, the tiny kitchen, the well-worn lime-green couch – and notice that nothing had really changed. Then there was the sound of the key fumbling in the door. I thought it would be Fezziwig coming home, or his sister, who must have inherited the room. But it wasn't either of them. Once again, the apartment had been lent out.

The door opened, and in swept the two boys I knew

as Tiny and Tim. Both had dressed up for the occasion, wearing ties and well-polished shoes, as well as jackets that each had a flower peeping from under the lapel. Both seemed to rejoice in being so gallantly attired, and to match so well. Tiny was the bearer of Fezziwig's keys, while Tim held bags of groceries in his arms.

"Our very own place," Tiny said, looking around as if they'd been granted a palace.

"Our very own," Tim echoed, putting the groceries down and swirling to take everything in.

Tiny plunged through Fezziwig's cabinets in search of pots and pans, while Tim lined up the ingredients for a feast along the small kitchen counter. They looked for any possible reason to touch each other, and when they couldn't find one, they touched each other anyway. Such giddy proximity. Such ready affections. All hesitation, all fear had been banished from the room.

I could only see it because I was invisible. If I'd been there, it wouldn't have happened the same way. I'd never seen it before, because the last time it had happened, I'd been inside of it.

There was only one knife in the drawer, so as Tiny

cut scallions, carved tofu, and sliced mushrooms, Tim sang to him. At first, silly songs – teasing ditties, rewritten pop songs. But then Tim launched into an old Sam Cooke song – *darling, you send me* – his voice an exquisite baritone usually kept hidden under his shy soul. The whole room seemed to sway in time. Tiny put down his knife and stopped to look at Tim with such love I could barely watch it. Then he smiled, set the gas burner alight, and began to cook.

Basking in luxurious thoughts of sage and onion, Tim danced around the table, clearing it off and then unveiling a tablecloth from the bottom of one of the grocery bags, as well as two long candlesticks, each the color of blue marbles. He floated his love to Tiny in the shape of Sam Cooke's tune as he lit each flame and folded each napkin in the shape of a valentine heart.

Tim took off his jacket and placed it on the back of his chair. Then he walked over and removed Tiny's jacket, gliding it off Tiny's shoulders even as Tiny stirred over the stove. Soon the two boys' jackets were sitting across from each other at the table, while the two boys pressed close in the steam heat of the kitchen.

As Tiny added spices and soy to his saucepan, Tim whispered things I couldn't hear, his hand placed lightly on Tiny's back, just to be there.

After many minutes of this, Tiny asked, "And how does little Tim feel?"

"As good as gold," said Tim. "And better." After a pause, he continued, "Sometimes when I'm sitting by myself so much, I have the strangest thoughts. Like today, when we were at the supermarket. I hoped that everyone saw us together. I thought, *Let's show them what love is really about.*"

Tim's voice was tremulous when he told Tiny this, and trembled even more when he said how happy he was.

"Right now," he said. "This is everything. I never thought. . . ."

"I never thought," Tiny echoed, putting the food aside and holding Tim close. "But I always knew."

They held like that for a moment longer, then Tiny said, "You get the grog."

Tim, turning up the cuffs of a shirt that didn't quite fit him yet, set about making some hot mixture of punch, putting it on the stove to simmer. Tiny, meanwhile, dressed the plates with flourishes of food. It smelled wonderful.

From the looks on their faces, you might have thought that tofu was the rarest of all meals, an unfeathered phenomenon to which the most luxurious of truffles were merely trifles. Tiny and Tim acted like the only two chefs, the only two waiters, and the only two customers in the most romantic restaurant ever devised. They did not sit across from each other, but instead shared the two sides of a corner, as if the table's length would have been too far apart. Their words to each other fell like grace, and then there was a breathless pause, as Tiny and Tim turned their attention to the food, the smell of it and the sight of it and its sheer existence making them murmur in delight.

I had forgotten this about love: how the simple things – the turn away, the turn towards – could be so complicated, and how the complicated things – the stolen night, the right words – could be so simple.

Tim said he didn't believe there was ever such a meal

cooked. Its tenderness and flavor, size and cheapness, were all admired. Completed by wine and a side of mashed potatoes, it was a sufficient dinner for two boys in love. They talked about the day, and about the days, and their words had the comfort and rhythm of a familiar song.

I missed her so much.

Every now and then, Tiny would turn from the table and tinker with ingredients in the kitchen nook. First there was flour and water and eggs. Then the spices and the sugar. Tim cleared the plates and prepared a new set, clearly anticipating what was to come.

"Don't look," Tiny said, too nervous to have Tim bear witness as the dessert was removed from the stove.

Tim sneaked a peek and cried, "Awesome!" The dessert was out of the oven and the room was filled with a smell like freshly clean laundry. With a smile, Tiny turned to display the dessert in his oven-mitted hands – it looked like a speckled cannonball, so hard and firm, blazing in a moat of ignited brandy, and garnished with two wedding-cake grooms stuck into the top.

"Oh, wonderful!" Tim said, and it was clear that he regarded it as the greatest success achieved by Tiny since they first came together.

"I'm not so sure I used the right amount of flour –" Tiny started to sputter, but Tim shushed him with a kiss.

I watched as the dinner was done, feeling so happy

and so sad. Soon the cloth was cleared and the fire lit. The grog was tasted and considered perfect, and apples and oranges were put on the table, along with handfuls of candy hearts. Then Tiny and Tim pulled the couch up to Fezziwig's fireplace, their arms forming a circle of two. As the golden goblets cooled at their feet and the fire sputtered and crackled in the grate, Tim proposed:

"A happy Valentine's Day to us, my dear. You're a blessing to me, Tiny."

"And you're a blessing to me, every day," Tiny replied.

Tim held Tiny's hand in his, as if he wanted to keep him always at his side, and dreaded that he might be taken from him.

"Spirit," I said, with an interest I hadn't felt since Marly had died, "tell me if Tiny and Tim will stay together."

"I see a vacant seat," replied the Ghost, "and empty arms. A heart without an owner, carefully reserved. If these shadows remain unaltered by the future, their love will die."

"No!" I cried. "You can't let that happen."

"If these shadows remain unaltered by the future, none other of my kind will find them like this. But are you so surprised?" The Ghost looked me straight in the eye. "Remember – they could plant fields of carnations for each other, and that won't prevent what's going to happen. Maybe Tim will find someone more attractive than Tiny. He'll cheat on him. He'll lie to him. He'll swear that it's love. Or maybe Tiny will leave Tim in a different way. He'll grow distant. He'll become a mystery Tim can't solve. Or maybe something else will intervene. Tiny will need Tim more than Tim can bear. It will be too much, and because it's too much, they'll know that they never really made it *in* love. They couldn't push far enough to be *in*."

I hung my head to hear my own words quoted by the Spirit, and was overcome with remorse and grief. I'd been hurt, yes – but I'd never meant to become hurtful. I didn't want to close down anyone but myself.

The Ghost continued. "You must ask yourself this: Will you decide when love's going to work and when it isn't? You have been pronouncing too much and feeling too little."

I bent before the Ghost's words and looked down at the ground. But I looked back up quickly when I heard my own actions suddenly recounted.

"That guy in the hallway was so horrible!" Tiny said.

"Totally!" Tim agreed, reddening. "I wish I had him here. I'd give him a piece of my mind to feast upon, and I hope he'd have a good appetite for it."

"My dear," was Tiny's mild answer, "I'm sure he has his own issues. Let's drink to him."

"Drink to such an odious, stingy, hard, unfeeling person!"

"Yes," Tiny said. "Because nobody is that way without a reason."

My body was shaking. Tiny picked up his glass . . . and Tim would not. One brief, frozen moment. The smallest of fractures.

Then Tim raised his glass and said, "I'll drink to him for your sake, and the day's. Not for his."

They drank, but it was the first part of their evening that had no warmth in it. The mere mention of me had cast a dark shadow on the party, which was not dispelled for minutes.

After it passed away, they were ten times happier than before, from the mere relief of my presence being done with. They reveled in being alone together, of having a place to themselves. Tim looked thoughtfully at the fire as they spoke of being with each other, deliberating how to spend this newfound time together. Tiny talked about how he meant to lie in bed tomorrow morning for a good long rest at Tim's side, how even if this had been February 15th or November 14th, it would still be a holiday to him. All this time, the chestnuts and the remnants of the pudding were passed back and forth, and by and by they sang together – songs about snow, songs about lost children found, songs about putting a little love in their hearts.

There was nothing incredibly glamorous in this. They were not an extraordinarily handsome couple. Their clothes didn't quite fit, and probably came from the Salvation Army. But they were happy, grateful, pleased with each other, and contented with the time; even as they faded, sprinkled brightly by the Spirit's torch, I couldn't take my eyes off of them.

By this time it was dark outside, and snowing pretty

heavily. As the Spirit and I went along the streets, the brightness of the lights in the kitchens, parlors, and all sorts of rooms was wonderful. Here, the glow showed preparations for a cozy dinner; there, a bedroom's deep-red curtains were about to be drawn by a half-naked pair of lovers. Here were shadows on the window blinds of guests assembling, and there a group of pretty girls, hooded and Ugg-booted and all chattering at once, tripping off lightly to some near neighbor's house where woe would befall the single guy who saw them enter – they were artful witches, and they knew it.

The Ghost clearly lived for this kind of night. She sparkled and opened to every person we passed. Everything within her reach was touched by this outpouring of love, this embrace of life.

For a moment – just a moment – that reach seemed to stretch past our town, across the entire globe. Like she was showing me how far and wide she could go. Like she was trying to make me a part of it again. I saw: the cheerful company assembled around a glowing fire in a dark and desolate stretch of the desert, where an old man sang a song of love to an old woman and their children and their children's children and the children a generation beyond that; a ship in the middle of the sea, where a young man lost himself in his pen, feverishly recording every detail of his longing for someone left behind; then the depths of a dreadful cavern, where two men joined their hands over the rough table at which they sat. I was inside the thoughts of soldiers at war, inside the hopes of nervous boys and giddy girls getting ready for a dance, inside the breath separating a yes from a no. And the Ghost was in every place, spreading the dust that came to look like life itself. The most common thing. Love was everywhere because life was everywhere.

As these images raced before my eyes, as I was being shown all these things, I was surprised to hear a hearty laugh. It was a much greater surprise to recognize it as my best friend's, and to find myself in the bright, dry, gleaming living room of his house, with the Spirit standing smiling by my side, looking at the same friend with an approving look.

"But this is an anti-Valentine party!" I said. "Are

you sure you belong here?"

"Oh, I feel especially welcome here," the Ghost replied.

"Ha, ha!" Fred laughed. "Ha, ha, ha!"

I didn't know anyone more blessed in a laugh than Fred. It was a laugh that came from the tip of his toes, gaining force and soul as it traveled through his body and out into the world in mirthful bursts. There wasn't anything fake about it; it was an amusement park ride of a laugh, and when it appeared, you wanted to jump on board.

It made me want to believe that in a world where there's disease and sorrow, there's still nothing as irresistibly contagious as laughter and good humor. When Fred laughed this way, holding his sides, rolling his head, and twisting his face into ridiculous contortions, the rest of the people in the room laughed as heartily as he did.

"Ha, ha! Ha, ha, ha, ha!"

"He said that love was *humbug*, I swear!" Fred cried. "He believed it, too!"

"'Humbug'? Is that what he's come to – 'humbug'?"

Sarah chimed in indignantly. She never held anything back; we were all subject to the full brunt of her opinions.

I will say this, though – there was certainly a sunny look in her eyes at this moment. She was very pretty, exceedingly pretty as she laughed, with a dimpled, surprised-looking face. For the first time, I saw her as Fred might have seen her – altogether something you would have called provoking. And, perhaps, good enough for my friend.

She was dressed in black – they were *all* dressed in black for the anti-Valentine party. Fred and Sarah and some of the other members of the group of friends – lackadaisical Topper, goth-shaded Teresa, red-threaded Lucy, existentialist Catie, pothead Charlie, and Sarah's two sophomore sisters – one plump, one thin – whose names I always forgot.

The room was a marvel of anti-Valentine spirit. Besides the black clothing, black drapes had been placed over the windows, giving everything a funereal charm. The television showed a horror movie on mute. Cupid cutouts had been placed around the room, shooting one another with arrows, each tip bloodily piercing angelic flesh. For food, someone had scratched off the faces of a package of candy hearts, and had written on other words instead: DESPAIR, HEARTBREAK, U R 2 DUM, LUV SUX, DON'T CALL ME, and so on. A black-iced cake in the shape of a valentine had already been cut to pieces. A piñata the shape of a rose awaited bursting.

Fred, who'd been the first to laugh, was also the first to stop. "He acts like a bitter old man," he said. "That's the truth. And he hasn't been much fun to be with lately. But he's hurting, you know. He's closed off so much that he doesn't even remember what he was like before, or how happy he can be. He's forgotten how to be a friend and won't let anyone remind him."

"I have no patience for him anymore," Sarah said. "You'd think he was the only one hurting." I could see some of the friends nodding. Agreeing.

"That's not fair," Fred said. "I feel sorry for him. I couldn't be angry with him if I tried. Who suffers when he acts so grim? He does, always. He won't hang out with us anymore and what's the consequence? I mean, it's not like we're the best Valentine's dates."

"I think we are!" Sarah interrupted. Everybody else said the same.

"Well, I'm glad you think so," Fred said, leaning over to kiss her. "What do *you* say, Topper?"

Topper had clearly gotten his eye on one of Sarah's sisters, for he answered that a single guy was a wretched outcast, who had no right to express an opinion on Valentine's Day. Sarah's sister – the plump one wearing a black lace dress, not the thin one with black-dyed roses in a corsage around her wrist – blushed.

"I was only going to say," Fred continued, "that the only thing that comes out of Ben's not joining us is that he loses any chance of having fun. And a little fun could do him some good. I'm sure our company has to be better than the company he can find in his own thoughts – even if those thoughts are in the past, with Marly. Because we're the ones who are here. I don't think he realizes how much we miss her too. Maybe he's unable to let himself see that. Maybe he really *has* given up. But I'm not going to give up on him. I'm going to give him chance after chance after chance, and maybe one day it will finally click, and he'll be back with us again. Because, you know, I miss him too. He may rail at love till he dies, but he can't help thinking better of it if we all keep loving him, if we all keep saying, 'Ben, how are you?' If we keep letting him know we're here, and that we're going to be here. We have to shake him. We have to get him back."

Nobody laughed now. It was as if they could feel me in the room. No. It was as if they could feel my absence. And her absence.

He had said her name. But not easily.

I wanted to be there then. Not to laugh. Not to be a participant. But to pull Fred aside and say – what? Thank you?

After a moment, Fred clearly sensed that the mood had grown too somber, so he unveiled a death-black punch that must have taken some serious brewing, and ladled it out as other people grabbed for cake and candy.

Catie went over to the stereo and soon the room was filled with music. The theme was adhered to – only the sadder love songs would be broadcast tonight: The Cure with no sense of a cure, breakup breakdowns and long-player longings. But music is music, no matter what the subject matter, and soon there was singing and swaying along. After a third glass of punch, Topper was especially vocal, growling away in the bass as Sarah's lacier sister harped and harped around him. Next came a banal boy-band ballad that we all loved to hate and hated that we loved – a mere nothing you might learn to whistle in two minutes. They all danced around, mocking the words and the dance moves from the video with unrestrained glee.

Watching them, hearing this, thinking about what the Ghost had shown me, I softened more and more, and thought that if I had kept listening to music after Marly died, if I had given in to it the way my friends were giving in to it now, then maybe I might not have buried my sense of kindness and friendship when Marly had been buried. She had always loved to dance like this, and that had become my reason for not doing it after she was gone. Now I realized it should have been my reason for keeping hold of it, for continuing.

But maybe it was too late. I still felt too far gone.

After a while the party shifted to old games like Twister and Boggle, because we all knew it was good to act like children sometimes. Then a blindfold was created out of Lucy's black scarf, and someone suggested a game of Blindman's Bluff. Topper was first to go, and I no more believed he was really blind than I believed he had eyes in his boots. The whole thing seemed to be set up, with Fred and Sarah grinning devilishly as they spun him around. (The Ghost of Love Present seemed pleased, as well – she could barely keep her hand away from her torch.) The way Topper went after the plump sister in the lace outfit was an outrage. Knocking down the fire irons, tumbling over the chairs, bumping against the stereo, smoothing himself among the drapery – wherever she went, there he was. He wouldn't catch anybody else. If you fell up against him on purpose (and some of our friends did), he faked an attempt to seize you, and then instantly sidled off in the direction of the sister. She often cried out that it wasn't fair, and it really wasn't. And when, at last, he caught her – when, in spite of all her rapid flutterings past him, he got her into a corner from whence there was no escape – well, then his conduct became even worse. He pretended not to know her, and that it was necessary to touch her hair and her hand and her neck in order to figure out her identity. I'm sure she told him what she thought of it all when the blindfold was passed to the next player and the two of them were so very confidential together, behind the curtains.

Sarah sat down in a large chair with a footstool in the snug corner where the Ghost and I stood. She called for a game of Charades, and soon two teams had been produced. Sarah was an ace at Charades, and of course volunteered herself as the first performer of clues. She held up two fingers, and her team cried, "Two words." Then she began to circle her arms widely.

"Propellers!"

"It's two words, Charlie."

"Plane propellers!"

"Ferris wheel!"

"A clock gone haywire!"

Sarah shook her head. Paused. Then pretended to sing.

"Organ grinder!"

"Player piano!"

"The Fat Lady Spins!"

"*Two words*, Charlie!"

Sarah shook her head. Then she began to shake an invisible skirt.

I got it.

"*Moulin Rouge!*" I cried. "The windmill. Singing. *Moulin Rouge!*"

But of course nobody could hear me. I had to wait two more clues – a movie projector, then a very strange rendering of the Eiffel Tower – before Lucy guessed it.

I got better and better as each person stood to act out the words. *One Hundred Years of Solitude. Sixteen Candles. Jagged Little Pill. Blue's Clues.* I was reading my friends' body language so well. I was knowing them.

If only they could see me.

I looked to the Ghost, who seemed greatly pleased to find me in such an energized mood. Sensing our time was running out – and wanting to take advantage of her good favor – I begged like a boy to be allowed to stay until the party was over.

"Time is short," came the reply.

"But here's a new game!" I said. "A half hour, Spirit! Please!"

It was Twenty Questions, and Fred was the one who had to think of something, and the rest had to find out what it was, with him only answering their questions yes or no. The barrage of drunken questioning elicited from him that he was thinking of an animal (as opposed to a vegetable or mineral), that it was a live animal, a disagreeable animal (it took him a while to answer this one), a savage animal (as opposed to cuddly), an animal that growled and grunted sometimes, and talked sometimes, and lived in town, and walked about the streets, and wasn't made a show of, and wasn't led by anybody, and didn't live in a menagerie, and was never killed in a market, and was not a horse, or an ass (more hesitation here), or a cow, or a bull, or a tiger, or a dog, or a pig, or a cat, or a bear. At every fresh question that was put to him, Fred burst into a fresh roar of laughter and was so inexpressibly tickled that he was obliged to get up off the sofa and stamp. At last the plump sister (having emerged from behind the curtain with quite an unlaced expression), fell into a similar state and cried out:

"I know what it is, Fred! I know what it is!"

"What is it?" cried Fred.

"It's your friend Ben!"

"That's not fair!" Charlie protested. "When we asked 'Is it a bear?' you should have said yes!"

Most of the others – even Sarah – groaned and protested at that. Although I had to admit to myself that the description wasn't that far off from what I'd let myself become.

"C'mon," Fred said, "it's not Ben. And he's far from a bear. I think it's time to drink to his health. Here is a glass of punch ready to our hand at the moment, and I say, To Ben!"

"To Ben!" everyone cheered.

"Right," said Fred. "A Happy Valentine's Day to our old friend, wherever he is. He wouldn't take it from me, but may he have it, nevertheless. Cheers, friend!"

I raised an imaginary glass and toasted him back. I had become so light of heart that I would have thanked everyone in a much lengthier speech if the Ghost had given me the time. But the whole scene dissolved in the breath of the last word spoken by my best friend, and the Spirit and I were traveling once again.

I missed them immediately. Missed them like a minor-key version of missing her.

I knew, however, that I could not go back. The Spirit had many more places to go. We saw so much and went so far, always with a happy end. The Spirit stood beside sickbeds, bringing relief. We went to foreign lands, but there was always the feeling of home. Struggling people were made patient in their greater hope by the dust from the Spirit's wand; the poor found richness. In homeless shelter, hospital, and jail – anyplace where misery was common and the door had not been barred or locked against the Spirit – she left her blessing and taught me her lessons.

I paid attention.

It was a long night, if it was only one night – I had my doubts about this, because the day appeared to be condensed into the space of time we spent together. It was strange, too, that while I looked and felt exactly the same, the Ghost grew older, clearly older. I had noticed it in passing, but didn't bring it up until we stood together in an anonymous open space. The Spirit's hair was now gray.

"Are spirits' lives so short?" I asked.

"My life on this globe is very brief," replied the Ghost. "It ends tonight."

"Tonight!"

"Tonight at midnight. The time is drawing near."

Chimes fell through the air to ring three quarters past eleven.

I stood and stared at the Spirit, not ready for her to go. Something strange stirred where her feet touched the ground.

"Forgive me if I'm totally out of place here," I said, looking intently at her robe, "but there seems to be a foot . . . or a claw, maybe . . . sticking out from under your skirt. And I don't think it's yours."

"It might be a claw for the flesh there is upon it," was the Spirit's sorrowful reply. "Look here."

From the foldings of her robe, she brought two children – truly wretched, horribly frightful children. They knelt down at her feet and clung to the outside of her garment. I wanted to turn away.

"Look!" the Ghost insisted.

They were a boy and a girl. Yellow, meager, ragged, scowling, wolfish, scared. They should have been so full of youth and joy, but instead it was as if a stale and shriveled hand had pinched and twisted them, pulling them into shreds.

I started back, appalled. I couldn't even pretend to like them, or understand them. The Spirit clearly wanted there to be some connection between us. But what?

"Are they yours?" I asked.

"They are humankind's," said the Spirit, looking down upon them. "And they cling to me. This boy is Isolation. This girl is Want. Beware them both, and everything like them, but most of all beware this boy, for Doom is going to be written on his brow unless something's done. Do everything you can do to stop it!

"Fight the desire to remain apart and wanting. And

if you try to keep others apart and wanting, know that you make it worse. Have *compassion*, I tell you!"

"Can't somebody help them?" I asked.

"But *you* don't want to have *anything to do with anyone else*!" the Spirit replied, turning on me for the last time with my own words. "As far as you're concerned, *nobody else exists*! That, more than anything, will lead you to your own doom."

I was about to ask *"My doom?"* when the bell struck twelve and the Ghost disappeared. I looked all around, but couldn't find her anywhere. As the last stroke ceased to vibrate, I remembered Marly's predictions and, lifting up my eyes, beheld a third, solemn Phantom, draped and hooded, coming like a mist along the ground toward me.

STAVE IV
THE LAST OF THE SPIRITS

THE PHANTOM SLOWLY, GRAVELY, SILENTLY APPROACHED.
When it came near me, I bent down on my knees,
surrendering to the gloom and mystery scattered in the air.

This Spirit was shrouded in a deep black garment that
concealed its head, its face, its form, and left no part of
it visible except for one outstretched hand. If it hadn't
been for this, it would have been difficult to separate it
from the darkness that surrounded it.

Tall and stately, it came beside me and filled me
with a solemn dread. I waited for it to speak ... but
it didn't speak. I waited for it to move further ...
but it didn't move.

"Are you the third Ghost?" I asked. "Has Marly sent you?"

The Spirit didn't answer, but pointed onward with its hand.

"You are about to show me shadows of the things that have not happened yet, but will happen in the future," I said. "Right?"

The upper portion of the Spirit's garment was contracted for an instant in its folds, as if the Spirit had inclined its head. This was the only answer I received. I had no idea if I was in the past, present, or future.

Although I'd grown used to the idea of being accompanied by ghosts, I feared this new silent shape so much that my legs trembled, and I found that I could barely stand. The Spirit paused a moment, as if it had seen the state I was in and was giving me time to recover.

This was worse. It was horrible to know that, behind the dusky shroud, there were ghostly eyes intently fixed upon me, while I couldn't see anything but a spectral hand and one great heap of black, no matter how hard I looked.

I had to remember that Marly had sent me this Ghost. This was the only fact that could lessen my fear.

"Ghost," I said, "I fear you more than any phantom I have seen. But since I know Marly sent you to do me some good, and since I plan to change my ways now, I will do what you want me to and I'll be thankful for it. So please – won't you speak to me?"

No reply. The hand kept pointing straight in front of us.

"The night is almost over," I continued, "and I know that time is precious to me. So just tell me where you need me to go and I'll go there."

The Phantom moved away as it had come toward me. I followed in the shadow of its robe.

We scarcely seemed to enter the high school; instead the building sprung up around us and encompassed us all on its own. There we were, in the heart of it, in the main hallway, walking among the students as they swung their backpacks and talked in groups and looked at their watches and worried about being late to class. I had seen this often enough.

The Spirit, much to my surprise, led us inside the girls' bathroom on the second floor. There was a little knot of girls in front of the mirror, and the Spirit pointed to them. They were unfamiliar to me – ninth graders, perhaps? I listened to their talk.

"No," said a pouty girl with a monstrous chin. "I don't know much about it. I only know that someone died."

"When?" inquired another girl, fixing her lipstick.

"Last night, I think."

"Why, what was the matter?" asked a third, taking a cigarette out of her large purse.

"God knows," said the first with a yawn.

"Friends?" asked a red-faced girl with a big zit on her nose, which she was desperately trying to cover with powder.

"Not me – that's all I know," said the girl with the large chin, yawning again.

This pleasantry was received with a general laugh.

"It's likely to be a very bogus funeral," said the same speaker. "I mean, who's going to go to it?"

"I don't mind going if they have food after," said

the girl with the zit on her nose. "I'll go if there's food."

Another laugh.

"Well, I'm the least interested, let me tell you," said the first speaker, "because I don't believe in all the lies people tell at those things, and I'm on a diet. But I'll go if that's the thing to do. I think I vaguely remember us crossing paths – in the halls, you know. Which is more than most people can say. From the halls, you know."

My blood was boiling by this time – it was the worst of everything I remembered from Marly's death. The people who were so unaffected, who acted like it was inconsequential – a bother, even. The girl *was* slightly familiar to me now – Marly and I probably *had* passed her in the halls. I wanted to shake her. I wanted to yell at her and tell her everything Marly had meant.

I looked to the Spirit for explanation. Why had it brought me here? Why now? To make me sad again about Marly? What did that prove? That sadness had been the only thing I had known, and even though I now realized more, it wasn't as if the sorrow had been erased.

Was I really going to have to relive those most awful days? Wasn't this supposed to be the future? Or was this supposed to mean that I'd always be stranded?

The Spirit glided back into the hall. Its finger pointed to two guys meeting. I knew them – they were two years younger than me, although they seemed a little older now. They both worked on the school newspaper, and I'd always made a point of getting along with them.

"How are you?" said one.

"How are you?" said the other.

"Well!" said the first. "I guess things came to their inevitable conclusion, didn't they?"

"So I'm told," returned the second. "Cold, isn't it?"

"It's February. You aren't a skater, are you?"

"No. No. Too many other things going on, you know? Anyway – I should get to class."

Not another word. That was their meeting, their conversation, and their parting.

I didn't know why the Spirit was leading me into conversations that were so trivial. There had to be something I was missing, and I tried to figure out what it was. It seemed strange for them to talk about Marly that way. But if not that, then what? What was the "inevitable conclusion"? Had someone else died? For some reason, I immediately thought of Tiny and Tim – but why?

I knew there was supposed to be a moral here. I knew I would round the corner at some point and I would see myself – past, present, or future. Seeing how this self acted would give me the clue I'd missed, and would give me the easy solution to the Spirit's riddles.

I scoured the halls to find myself, but there was another kid at my locker, and though it was the usual time of day to switch books, I saw no likeness of myself near, or among the waves that poured from the classrooms.

Then I saw Tiny. And the first thing I recognized was that he wasn't as tiny anymore. So this had to be the future. Tiny was alone at his locker, shoveling books inside from his bag.

He looked . . . empty. Older. Alone.

I looked inside the locker and saw a bouquet of dead flowers hanging upside down. As if responding to my gaze, Tiny ripped them down and threw them in the nearest trash can.

I looked around for Tim.

But he wasn't there. And the longer he wasn't there, the more I worried.

Could it have been . . . ?

Please no, I thought. *Please.*

At that moment, Tim appeared at the end of the hall. I was relieved – so relieved. Then he grew closer and I could see how different he was. Gaunt. Hollow. His eyes nearly dead. Zoned out. Gone.

At first Tiny didn't see him, and then he did. He fought the sight, the desire to see. He tried to turn away, but he couldn't. As Tim came closer, Tiny turned to him. I could see words ready on his lips. But Tim just walked by. No acknowledgment. No care. Nothing. As if Tiny were invisible alongside me.

Tiny turned his face to his locker and slumped down a little, defeated. He stared straight into the shadow and tried not to cry.

"No," I said. *"No."*

Quiet and dark, the Spirit stood beside me with its outstretched hand. I sensed that the unseen eyes were looking at me keenly. It made me shudder and feel very cold.

We left school and went into an obscure part of town, to a building I had never seen before. We were on faceless streets now – strip malls and fast-food places and business complexes. We entered through the back door of this building, into an office that looked like chaos itself. This was not the area where customers would be greeted; this was the back room. Secrets that few would like to scrutinize were bred and hidden in mountains of paperwork, file folders spewing out filled-out forms. Glossy photos of coffins were scattered everywhere. Sitting among the wares, by a charcoal stove made of old bricks, was a gray-haired man who looked about seventy. He smoked his pipe like he had all the time in the world.

The Spirit and I came into the presence of this man just as a woman with an urn of coffee slunk into the office. She had barely entered when another woman carrying an urn to be used for ashes came in too, followed closely by a man in faded black.

"Are we ready?" said the old man by the stove. "Shut the door for a sec, will ya? Ah, how it skreeeeks! There ain't such a rusty bit of metal in the place as its own hinges, I believe, and I'm sure there's no such old bones here as mine. Especially not our current resident, ha ha! We're all suitable to our calling, we're well matched. Are we getting a crowd, Mrs. Dilber?"

"Some," the woman with the coffee urn said. "There're usually more when they're this young."

"Well, he did top himself, right?" replied the old man. "That always makes 'em nervous. You can get a better deal with the family, they're so shaken. Right, Joe?"

"Sure thing," the other man said. "Most expensive casket, no questions asked."

"Oh, how people squander," Mrs. Dilber said.

"Well, isn't that appropriate in this case?" the woman with the urn for ashes said. "He certainly did his share of squandering. Nineteen years old!"

"It's the truest word that ever was spoke," Mrs. Dilber testified. "It's a judgment on him."

"I wish it was a little heavier judgment," replied the woman. "And maybe that he'd been alive to hear it."

"But then where would our business be!" the old man exclaimed.

"I could use those extra years he had," the woman said.

I listened to this dialogue in horror. Had they no respect for the dead? Or for the living? Didn't they care at all? Their attitude disgusted me – how could they value life so little? I felt like they were about to sell the corpse, not bury it.

I was so mad that their words had little time to sink in.

But once I quieted their conversation, one line echoed:

Well, he did top himself, right?

This filled me with horror too.

And I was glad it filled me with horror. Because there had been times when – yes, when I had wanted to die. More and more so, until this night. It wasn't that I thought I could be reunited with Marly – I held no hope for that. But there were moments when I couldn't go on without her. It was just too hard. Every single thing was just too hard.

I wouldn't have done it. I hadn't done it.

"Spirit!" I said, shuddering from head to toe. "I see, I see. I could have ended up like this guy. There were moments when I went in that direction. But still –"

I recoiled in terror, for the scene had changed, and now I almost touched a gurney – a bare, uncurtained rolling cot on which, beneath a ragged sheet, there lay something covered up that, though it was speechless, announced itself in an awful language.

We were in the same building, in a different room. This room was very dark, too dark to be observed clearly, though I glanced around instinctively, anxious to know what kind of room it was. A pale light, rising in the air, fell straight upon the makeshift bed. On it, unwatched and lifeless, was the body of the deceased.

I looked at the Spirit, unwilling to look at the bed. But the Spirit's steady hand pointed insistently to the corpse's head. The cover was so carelessly adjusted that the slightest raising of it, the small movement of a finger on my part, would have shown the face. I thought about it, felt how easy it would be to do, how I longed to know for sure, but I had no more power to withdraw the veil than to dismiss the specter at my side.

I closed my eyes and thought:

Please, Death. I know you are standing beside me now. I know why we're both here. When the heart stops, you die. Love is everywhere that life is, and if there is no love for life, you die. Giving up on love is the same thing as giving up on life itself. What I did – what this person did – was wrong. Because something I loved was taken away from me, I gave up on everything else. It started as love, but that turned into life. But if I had loved, if I hadn't drawn apart from everything, you wouldn't be able to do this. I will change. I have already changed. I can lift myself back up. My heart still beats. I know what Marly would want me to do. If this body in front of me could be raised up now, his thoughts would no longer be so isolated from love. He gave up, but I won't.

"Spirit," I said, "this is a fearful place. When I leave here, I won't leave its lesson behind. Trust me. I'm ready to go now."

Still the Ghost pointed with an unmoved finger at the head.

"I understand you," I said. "And I would do it if I could. But I don't have the power, Spirit. I don't have the power."

Again it seemed to look upon me.

"It can't just be about me. Isn't there someone else who's hurt by this death?" I asked, quite agonized. "Show that person to me, Spirit. I beseech you!"

At first I saw my parents walking through our empty house. I couldn't watch. It was too much.

Then we were in Fred's bedroom. He was wearing

144

a formal white shirt and the pants from his only suit. He was looking in the mirror, trying to tie a black tie around his neck. His hands were shaking so much that he couldn't do it. He tied, then untied. Tied, then untied. With each attempt, he grew angrier and angrier. Cursing himself. Yelling in frustration. Tears forming in his eyes, falling down his cheeks.

"I can't do this," he said. "I can't."

The door opened and Sarah appeared. She was different now – her hair shorter, her makeup less pronounced. This was Sarah in college, a Sarah I didn't know. Fred turned to her with such despair, the tie half hung around his neck. She welcomed him into her arms, held him tight.

"I came as soon as I heard," she said.

"That bastard," Fred sobbed. "That stupid, stupid bastard."

"It's okay, it's okay," Sarah murmured.

"It's not."

Fred pulled away, tore at his tie again and tried to fix it.

"Topper and Lucy are already here," Sarah said. "Catie couldn't afford to fly back. But she said she was really sorry to hear it. Sorry for his family, and sorry for you too, because you were such a good friend."

"Not good enough," Fred said, his voice the absolute opposite of his laugh.

"Everybody knows you are," Sarah replied, leaning over his shoulders and taking the tie in her hands. "He got by us, though. We tried, and you tried the most. But he was never the same. We couldn't fix him; it was always up to him, and he didn't want to."

The tie was tied, the collar folded down.

"If Marly were here, she would be so mad at him," Fred said.

"We're all mad at him. Because we loved him."

"Why didn't he know?" Fred asked.

But there was no answer to that. None that they could give.

I didn't even know the answer anymore. It belonged to a different me.

The one who was now dead.

I just needed to hear it said. I needed the Spirit to tell me.

"Specter," I said, "I have a feeling that you're going to leave me soon. I know it, but I don't know how.

Tell me who it was that we saw lying dead."

The Ghost did not say anything, but conveyed me forward, until we reached an iron gate. I paused to look around before entering.

The churchyard. Walled in by houses and overrun with weeds, choked up with too much burying.

The Spirit stood among the graves and pointed down to one. I advanced toward it, trembling. The Phantom was exactly as it had been, but I dreaded that I saw new meaning in its solemn shape.

"Before I draw nearer to that stone," I said, "answer me one question. Are these the shadows of the things that will be, or are they shadows of the things that *may* be, only?"

Still the Ghost pointed downward to the grave by which it stood.

"I know a person can step on a path that, once he chooses to walk down it, will only lead to one end," I said. "But if you step off that path, the end will change, right? I can still change my path, can't I?"

The Spirit was as immovable as ever.

I crept forward, trembling as I went. Then, following

the finger, I read upon the stone of the neglected grave my own name, EBENEZER SCROOGE.

I cried out and fell to my knees, all of it now entirely real. The finger pointed from the grave to me, and back again.

"No, Spirit! Oh no, no!"

The finger was still there.

"Spirit!" I cried. "Listen to me! I am not the person I was. I will not be the person I was. Why show me this if I am past all hope?"

For the first time the hand appeared to shake.

"Please, Spirit," I pursued, falling down on the ground before it, refusing to give up, "I know you don't want to do this. You know I can change. You pity me. *Please tell me I can change my path*."

The hand trembled.

"I will love and be kind and be compassionate. I will live in the past, present, and future. The Spirits of all three shall strive within me. I will not shut out the lessons that you've taught me. Please – *tell me I can erase the writing on this stone*!"

In my agony I caught the spectral hand. It sought

to free itself, but I kept hold with all my strength. The Spirit, stronger yet, repulsed me.

Holding my hands up, I cried Marly's name over and over, praying my love for her could reverse my fate instead of ensuring it, knowing now that my love for her could also be my love for everything else. The Phantom's shape began to alter. Before my tear-filled eyes, it shrunk, collapsed, and dwindled into a bedpost.

STAVE V

THE END OF IT
AND THE
BEGINNING OF IT

AND THE BEDPOST WAS MY OWN. The bed was my own, the room was my own. Best and happiest of all, the time before me was all my own, to make amends in.

"I will live in the past, the present, and the future!" I repeated, scrambling out of bed. "The Spirits of all three shall strive within me. Oh, Marly! I say it on my knees, Marly. *On my knees!*"

I was so fluttered and so glowing with good intentions that my broken voice could scarcely match everything I wanted to say. I had been sobbing violently in my conflict with the Spirit, and my face was wet with tears.

Everything was so precious to me. The sheets that had fallen to the floor. The fireplace. The door to the world. *They are here*, I thought. *I am here.*

I was so giddy I nearly burst out of my clothes.

"I don't know what to do!" I exclaimed, laughing and crying in the same breath. I felt as light as a feather, as happy as an angel, as merry as a little kid. I wanted to whoop and holler. I wanted to let the world in again.

There was the door that Marly had come through. There was the corner where the Ghost of Love Present had sat. There was the window where I had seen the wandering spirits. It was all right, it was all true, and it had all happened.

I laughed.

It had been so long since I'd laughed with all my body, all my soul. It was a great laugh, the father of a long, long line of brilliant laughs.

"I don't know what day of the month it is," I said. "I don't know how long I have been among the Spirits. I don't know anything. I'm such a baby! Never mind. I don't care. I'd rather be a baby. Hello! Whoop! Hello, world!"

The belltowers rang out the lustiest peals I had ever heard. Clash, clash, hammer; ding, dong, bell! Bell, dong, dong, hammer, clang, clash! Oh, glorious, glorious!

I ran to the window, opened it, and put out my head. No fog, no mist; clear, bright, brilliant, stirring cold; cold that made the blood dance to my cheeks; golden sunlight; heavenly sky; sweet fresh air; merry bells. Oh, glorious! Glorious!

I saw the boy who lived next door riding his bike in his driveway.

"What's today?" I cried out to him.

"Eh?" returned the boy.

"What day is today?"

"Today?" replied the boy. "Why, Valentine's Day!"

"It's Valentine's Day," I said to myself. "I haven't missed it. The Spirits have done it all in one night. They can do anything they like. Of course they can." I yelled out to the boy, "Hey!"

"Hello!" he yelled back.

"Do you know the florist in town? The nice one?" I inquired.

"Of course," replied the boy.

"I need you to do me a favor. Can you go there and buy the biggest, most wonderful bouquet they have?"

"The one as big as me?" the boy asked. He was nine or ten at most.

"Yes!" I replied. "Can you carry it?"

"Are you paying?"

"I am!" I went to my wallet and wrapped up a few bills before dropping them down to him. "That should be enough," I said, "and you can buy Valentine's presents with the rest."

The boy was off like a shot.

I left the window open as I turned back to the room. I knew what I had to do first. And it was hard – harder than anything that had happened in the night, harder than anything I had imagined, because of all things, I had never imagined doing this.

Trembling, I slipped to my bottom drawer and took out my box of Marly's letters and trinkets. Even though I couldn't see her ghost, I could feel her in the room. I felt her watching as I read the letters, as I ran all the souvenirs over my palm. Smiling some. Crying.

Taking the past into my hands. Remembering it. And then putting it away.

I let go of my half of the chain. I felt it drop from me, and only the weight of it was gone, not Marly. Somehow I knew that the chain was unwinding from her as well. I was freeing us. I picked up her charm bracelet and rang the bell, hearing how small it was now, small and sad, sad but small. I knew she would never truly be gone, and that we would never truly be separated. But a chain wasn't the way to hold her. The bond that held us together was made of the same substance as a thought – intangible, invisible, and yet still as deeply there as anything else in the wide world.

The doorbell rang, and I ran downstairs to find the boy on my front step, his arms full of roses. He was laughing at the enormity of it, and I had to laugh too.

"Are they all for you?" he asked.

"They're for me to give away," I replied. He seemed satisfied by that answer, and so was I.

Before I closed the door, I took a long look at the door knocker, knowing as I did that I would love it for as long as I lived. I had scarcely looked at it before, but now I saw it had a very honest expression on its face.

"Happy Valentine's Day," I said to it.

It did not say anything back, but I chuckled anyway. Then I closed the door and sat down on the staircase, breathless and chuckling until I cried.

I hurried back upstairs to ready myself for my re-entry into the land of the living. Shaving was not an easy task, for my hand continued to shake, and shaving requires attention, even when you don't dance while you're doing it. But even if I'd cut the end of my nose off, I would have just put a Band-Aid on it and headed out anyway.

I dressed myself in my best clothes, including a red tie that Marly had bought me two Valentine's Days ago. Then, with the roses filling my arms, I headed out into the streets. The people were by this time pouring from their houses, as I had seen with the Ghost of Love Present. I regarded each of them with a delighted smile, remembering all of the love letters sailing through our town. I even managed to pass the snow-shoveling man as his wife came out to deliver her envelope. But I didn't stay; the moment was theirs, not mine.

People smiled when they saw the multitude of roses in my arms and, I hoped, when they witnessed the expression on my face. They wished me a happy day, and I wished it back upon them.

I had not gone far when I saw a group of girls heading in my direction – one who did not yet have a zit on the tip of her nose and one who did not yet need to fix her lipstick, but the third most definitely having a horrible chin. Their awful words of two years from now still echoed in my ears, but I knew what path lay straight before me, and I took it.

"My dear ladies," I said, bowing before them, "how do you do?"

"Do we, like, know you?" the pouty girl with the chin asked.

"No, but you'll remember me," I said, taking a rose out for each of them.

"Are you serious?" the red-faced girl currently without the zit asked.

"Yes. I just wanted to wish you a happy day."

The third girl's expression brightened as she took one of the roses. "That's so nice of you," she said. "Thanks."

"My pleasure," I replied, holding out the two remaining roses, which were soon taken.

"He was cute," one of them whispered after they had passed.

"Yeah, but probably psycho," another whispered back.

I kept walking until I hit Fezziwig's place. The spare key was exactly where I remembered it being. I knocked a few times, just in case. When there was no answer, I knew I still had a little time.

The apartment was just as I'd witnessed, awaiting the next arrival.

"Darling, you send me," I sang as I propped up roses in the coils of the silent stove.

"Darling, you do," I sang as I threaded roses through the handles of drawers and the logs in the fire.

Everywhere you looked, there were roses. The room itself had become a bouquet. And I left it for them, without a word. I didn't have a wand, but I could still do my best.

Once the key was safely returned to its hiding place, I headed back into town, looking for my friends' favorite things. My memory of Marly's favorites had always remained encyclopedic. But I was happily surprised to find that my instinct for the rest of our group hadn't disappeared in all of my sorrow. I bought four decks of cards and then created a deck entirely of hearts for Topper. For Catie, I bought a rainbow set of blank CDs and then sandwiched the red ones between two albums of old love songs. I found Charlie a red pipe, Lucy a red scarf. For Sarah, I bought a bottle of grenadine, so she could mix the Shirley Temples that I somehow remembered she loved.

Fred was the hardest – not because I didn't know what he wanted, but because nothing seemed like enough. I went from store to store to store, my mind drifting over the day. Then I realized what I would do. I bought a red frame and ran back home, taking Marly's shoebox out again. There was a snapshot of the three of us, taken during the happiest of times. I loved the photo dearly, and I knew it would hurt me to lose even a single captured moment with her. But I understood that Fred would know that as well, and he would know what I meant by giving it to him. It was time for us to share these things. It was time for me to try.

I went back into the streets as evening set. I watched the people hurrying to and fro, and was so glad to be one of them. Just the fact that they could see me brought such unbelievable happiness. I looked into the kitchens, up to the windows, and found that everything could yield me pleasure. I had never dreamed that any walk, that anything, could give me so much back.

I passed Fred's house a dozen times before I had the courage to go up and knock. I looked inside my bag at all of the red things I had brought; I knew they didn't fit the theme of the party, but I knew they fit its spirit.

I could hear the footsteps coming toward the door. I could hear the knob turning. And then I could see the surprise on Fred's face. The utter, joyful surprise.

"Ben!" he cried.

"Will you let me in, Fred?" I asked.

Without a word, he opened his arms and welcomed me back. And I let myself be drawn into the shape of our old friendship. He gripped tight and I gripped tighter. That was all we had to do.

"Look who's here!" he called out. When I entered the den, everybody cheered. I was at home in five minutes. It was just as I had seen it, but now I was a part of it. Everybody loved their gifts, and I fell into their running conversations like I'd never left them. The only tension came when we got to Charades – no one could understand how I guessed the answers so quickly.

It was a wonderful party, full of wonderful games, wonderful unanimity, and wonderful happiness. At the end we raised our glasses and toasted to Marly. I was not afraid to say her name, or to wish she was there. It felt right.

I made sure to be early to school the next day. I was relieved to see Tiny and Tim holding hands as they walked to Tiny's locker. They, of course, did not look at all relieved to see me. I nearly laughed from their scared expressions . . . but realized it was a joke that they weren't yet in on.

"I owe you both an apology," I began at once. "I was in an awful mood yesterday and I took it out on you. Everything I said was wrong. Your love is clearly real and entirely worthy. I was a fool to cast even the smallest shadow on it. I am so, so sorry."

Now they were looking at me even more strangely. This wasn't at all what they were expecting.

"It's okay," Tiny finally said.

"No need to apologize," Tim added.

"Of course there is," I told them, and apologized some more. Eventually, the conversation moved to Valentine's Day – both beamed when they told me what a spectacular time they'd had together. Soon I was offering to drive them places if they ever needed a ride, and they were eager to accept. I vowed that I would help them . . . and they, in unison, vowed they would help me too.

I hope I have been better than my word. I've tried to do it all, and infinitely more. To Tiny and Tim – who did not break up – I've been a friend and a means of escape. I've tried to be as good a friend and as good a person as our town has known, or any other city, town, or borough. Some people laughed to see the change in me, thinking me *too* compassionate and *too* kind. But I let them laugh, and paid no attention to them, for I felt wise enough now to know that nothing ever happens on this globe for good without some people having their fill of laughter at first. I knew that such people as these would be blind anyway to love. My own heart laughed, and that was quite enough for me.

I've had no further visitations from spirits, although I can always feel Marly near me. It's been said of me that I know how to love well, if any person alive can possess such knowledge. May that be truly said of us, and all of us.

It is all such a blessing – in the beginning, and the end, and the during.

THE END

THE AUTHOR AND ILLUSTRATOR WOULD LIKE TO ACKNOWLEDGE...

First and foremost, we would like to thank Charles Dickens, the illustrator John Leech, and whoever devised the concept of public domain. This novel is very much a remix, incorporating parts of the text and illustration from the original version of *A Christmas Carol*. (For more about this, please see the following Author's Note.) Dickens's work is nothing short of a marvel, and we're happy to have been able to borrow it for a little bit.

This book would not have existed without the

kernel from Lauri Hornik, and the illustrations would not have existed without a brunch Brian had with the amazing Susan Raboy. Thanks also go to Teresa Kietlinski for her inspired design, Sarah Weeks for transforming her apartment into a studio (and for being such a great all-round friend), and Natty Abbott and his friends for being willing subjects (and good sports).

We would be entirely remiss if we didn't thank "the boys" – David, Billy, Nico, and Nick, who spent hours upon hours hearing about this book, and who were encouraging all the way. Thanks as well to Nancy Hinkel, for her understanding; Rachel Cohn, for her insight; and to our families, for their constant support.

Finally, we would like to give garlands of gratitude to our magnificent editor, Nancy Mercado. She doesn't have an ounce of humbug within her, and needs neither wand nor spell to spread great joy and cheer.

Thank you all.

AUTHOR'S NOTE

This is very much a remix novel. While I've endeavored to create my own music, I've also sampled greatly from the story's original source. How, you might ask, did this come about?

The idea was not mine. Nancy and Lauri from Dial approached me to write "a Valentine's Day version of *A Christmas Carol.*" I was intrigued. I think they were expecting a romantic comedy (the Ghost of Boyfriends Past, etc.), and I initially assumed that was the direction I would go in. But then I decided to reread Dickens's original. I hadn't read it since ninth grade or so, and

I quickly realized that I'd let all of the other versions (from *Scrooged* to Scrooge McDuck) block out what Dickens really wrote. Reading *A Christmas Carol* anew, I was certainly struck again by how brilliant Dickens's writing is and how he somehow manages to capture not only the "holiday spirit" but the human spirit as well. But what really hit me this time was how heartbreaking the majority of the book is, as we see all that Scrooge has lost in his greed. Suddenly, romantic comedy didn't seem the obvious way to go.

The title came first. *Marly's Ghost.* Then I asked myself: Who's Marly? And the story slowly took shape in my mind.

For the actual writing, I sat with a copy of *A Christmas Carol* on my lap and went through it paragraph by paragraph, line by line, "translating" the original story into my new story, taking the original tune and turning it into a remix. Some lines stayed verbatim. Others twisted and turned into new meanings. Some of the scenes in the original novel were cut, but most of them stayed in some way.

Once I turned the last page of *A Christmas Carol* and

wrote the last line of my first draft, I put the original away. The more I revised and remixed, the more the story and music became my own. But Dickens is still there underneath every word – sometimes on the surface, sometimes deep below.

The same is true with the art. As I was writing, my friends Brian and David very patiently listened as I described each stage of my work-in-progress. Then they happened to go to London and discovered a copy of the original edition of *A Christmas Carol*. Brian was intrigued by John Leech's illustrations, and (with the encouragement of our friend Susan Raboy) decided to remix Leech's drawings in the same way that I was remixing Dickens's text. Most of the resulting pieces in this book are direct adaptations of the original art; the rest adapt Leech's look for new scenes.

I love the notion of spinning something new out of something already well-known. Remixing is a different kind of writing, but I've finished it with much satisfaction. This isn't really my book at all – it's shared with Charles Dickens, and Brian Selznick, and John Leech, and all the other versions that have come before, and all the other versions that will continue to appear. May Dickens's story always ring true, in whatever guise.

ABOUT THE AUTHOR

David Levithan lives in the best of times and the worst of times, the age of wisdom and the age of foolishness, the epoch of belief and epoch of incredulity, the season of Light, and the season of Darkness.

He has endeavored in this Ghostly little book to raise the Ghost of an Idea which shall not put his readers out of humor with themselves, with each other, with the season, or with him.

Whether he shall turn out to be the hero of his own life, or whether that station will be held by anybody else, time must show.

ABOUT THE ILLUSTRATOR

Brian Selznick is the award-winning illustrator of many books for children, including the Caldecott Honor book *The Dinosaurs of Waterhouse Hawkins* by Barbara Kerley, the Sibert Honor book *When Marian Sang* by Pam Muñoz Ryan, *The Doll People* and its sequel, *The Meanest Doll in the World*, both by Ann Martin and Laura Godwin, and many books by Andrew Clements, including the perennial bestseller *Frindle*. Brian has also written and illustrated *The Houdini Box* and *The Boy of a Thousand Faces*.

Brian lives in Brooklyn, New York. And so, as Tiny Tim observed, God Bless Us, Every One!

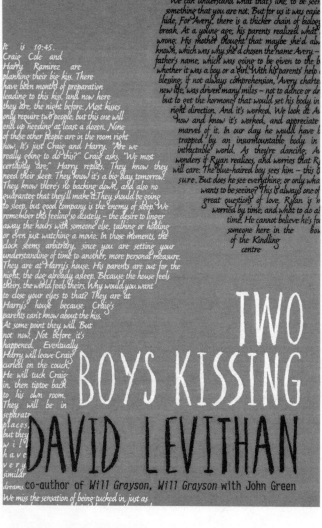

HOW THEY MET

AND OTHER STORIES

DAVID LEVITHAN

co-author of *Will Grayson, Will Grayson* with John Green

AN EXPLORATION OF THAT
WONDERFUL, COMPLEX, SIMPLE,
ADDICTIVE, VOLATILE, SCARY,
GLORIOUS THING CALLED LOVE.

NICK & NORAH'S INFINITE PLAYLIST

RACHEL COHN & DAVID LEVITHAN

TWO STRANGERS SHARE AN EPIC FIRST DATE, WITH A KILLER SOUNDTRACK, OVER ONE VERY LONG NIGHT IN NEW YORK.

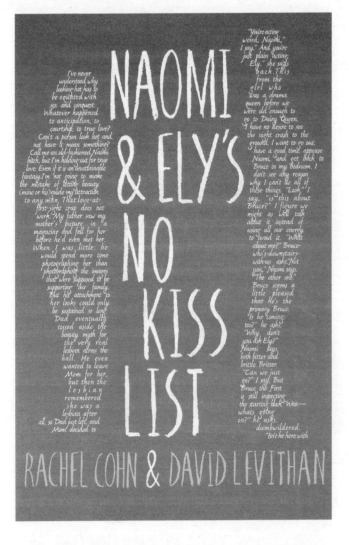

NAOMI & ELY'S NO KISS LIST

RACHEL COHN & DAVID LEVITHAN

ANY GREAT FRIENDSHIP CAN BE AS CONFUSING, TREACHEROUS, INSPIRING AND WONDERFUL AS ANY GREAT ROMANCE

EVERY DAY

DAVID LEVITHAN

EVERY DAY I AM SOMEONE ELSE.
I AM MYSELF – I KNOW I AM MYSELF –
BUT I AM ALSO SOMEONE ELSE.
IT HAS ALWAYS BEEN LIKE THIS.